HOMING IN

Marjorie Oludhe Macgoye

HOMING IN

MARJORIE OLUDHE MACGOYE

East African Educational Publishers
Nairobi

Published by
East African Educational Publishers Ltd
Brick Court
Mpaka Road/Woodvale Grove
Westlands
P.O. Box 45314
Nairobi, Kenya

ISBN 9966-46-547-2

Printed by
Kenya Litho Limited
Changamwe Road, P.O. Box 40775
Nairobi

Most of the proper names used in this book are common ones. The story is fictional and no reference is intended to any individual, except in the following cases:

Jos and Nellie Grant are so well known through the writings of their daughter, Elspeth Huxley, that one cannot ignore their presence at the given time and place.

Muchoka is named as the senior member of their farm staff.

Hector Munro, Lady Cole and Lady Farrar are all well known farmers.

RSM Okari and his party of returned prisoners of war are described in the newspapers of the time.

Trade names are taken from the press of the period.

Author

Chapter 1

Martha wheeled Mrs. Smith out to the gate. She was always a little anxious, would have liked to keep the old lady nearer the house within earshot while she cooked and tidied. But Ellen preferred the gate. "I want to see Angela as soon as she comes," she would say, and Martha would give in with a drawn smile and fuss around. There had been a time when Ellen thought the ayahs never fussed enough: she understood now that she herself had fussed far too much about the wrong things – white socks and homework instead of facing the future – and that she had never known the ayahs as she had known Martha. At least, she thought she knew her: how else would this intimate care and double dependence be tolerable? But at sixty-six it was only decent to admit that one knew less than one used to think. She had always told the schoolgirls not to be ashamed of confessing what they did not know: this was the gateway to learning. They looked at her, wide-eyed, civil, contemptuous. One of them, the niece of a teacher, Mrs. Banerjee, had betrayed her.

"Of course we want the students to have receptive minds," said Mrs. Banerjee, apropos of nothing, "but their esteem for us must not be damaged. We have a position to keep up." And at the end of term the headmaster droned, "We are fortunate in Kenya to have so many traditions of learning to draw on: this should enhance our authority and competence."

"What do you understand by the word 'enhance'?" Ellen had asked the next year's form three. The girls thought it had something to do with perfume or make-up. So much for Eng. Lit., but at least they read attentively what interested them.

Martha worried too much in Mrs. Smith's view. It was not as if she could not walk: she could walk quite well for short distances, but she must save her strength for occasions like her daughter's coming. She could get to the kitchen with her sticks and was sure she could light the paraffin stove so long as someone had filled it and put things out at table height. Not that she could stay alone in the house – she was honest enough to admit that. And it was necessary to give Martha something to do to preserve her self-respect.

Martha's self-respect – that was a new thought, and Ellen Smith was not quite able to cope with it. In the past, Martha would have been supervising her fields if not actually bringing in the harvest herself, but times had changed and she had no fields (as far as her employer knew) and no helpers either. Ellen no longer had a salary cheque, but there was a pension for the years of teaching and something from investments that came through the bank each month: Nigel had explained it to her but she did not now remember. Her own little cash-box was replenished at Christmas and on her birthday, and from this she could give something to Mrs. Mistri or Mrs. Banerjee when they called to buy her birthday cards and stamps and batteries for the radio, hairpins, stockings. Martha had to do the household shopping and was always careful to consult her – would she like sausages, fish, pineapple or plums now they were in season? But she did not give orders for the sugar and margarine, soap and tea and potatoes: they somehow appeared, just like the clean sheets and towels and underwear. And Martha would ask her, "Would you like the blue dress today? No, I have washed the flowered one, but there is the spotted one if you prefer it, or the dark red. We'll keep the two-piece nice for visitors, shall we?"

Martha was a treasure, and where else would she go, a hard-working widow with grown-up children? Ellen knew she was lucky compared to her own mother, and *she* had been lucky for her time: she always had a daily woman (well, twice a week, perhaps) and would have expected a resident maid as she grew older. But all the maids joined the ATS or something when the war came, and got new ideas. Mummy had managed somehow, though she had grown up to take home deliveries for granted and never (it seemed from family letters) got used to assembling her own goods in a supermarket. Here in Kenya small-holding neighbours brought milk and vegetables to the door, so different from the early days when the nearest European house was two miles off and no one had given her an introduction to other kinds of houses.

She was grateful to Martha but also proud, for Martha knowing decent Swahili and quite a lot of English, had grown to meet her employer's needs – in fact more so than Mrs. Smith knew, for the private language to which Martha responded was hardly English any more. The cracked sounds could hardly obey the precision of Ellen's thoughts, even when these were not submerged in the pictures that rolled around in her head.

They had enough to live on, though she had chosen to give up cooked breakfasts and having her hair done. This Ellen saw quite clearly, even now that her movements had become circumscribed and her memory capricious. She had memories of a life which overflowed the narrow channel left for it and made her happy to tilt the kaleidoscope and see the patterns glint and sparkle and reshape themselves. When the children were small one was disappointed that the toys broke or got lost so quickly, but back in one's own childhood a sunny afternoon had lasted so long that the treasured, brief possession seemed endless.

At her feet a piece of green glass glinted in the garden soil. She remembered wearing a dress of that rich, opaque green during her first winter teaching in the grammar school. Heavy cloths used to come in plain colours then, never patterned except with discreet lines or flecks, and you needed warm clothes, scurrying through draughty corridors to classrooms where hot water radiators hardly diminished the chill in the air. The glass must have come from a broken bottle. Bottles were everywhere, however far back in time or in whatever god-forsaken camping spot, accompanying man as soon as he learned to manufacture them and to trade. Bottles from the ocean depths of recovered wrecks, shards of glass setting off bush-fires, bottles shoved into babies' mouths, bottles wherever men went without their womenfolk, tripping Jack up against a faulty tractor, withdrawing him into the unimaginable fellowship of khaki uniforms. Ginger-beer bottles of her childhood with the marble revolving in the top - everything was real glass then, no concession for children till celluloid came and mothers worried unceasingly that it would catch fire. Green glass for harmless things, not the brown and blue of the surgery, but it seems that nothing is harmless any more. It is always bad for your heart or your liver or your teeth. In granny's day they would take out all your teeth to make you better, and leave you nipping delicately with bits of white porcelain, really more barbaric than any witch-doctor if they had but known. But English girls were taught to be more frightened of witch-doctors than of dentists.

Her brother Stanley might have got her over the fear of losing her teeth, but Stanley was a schoolboy when she went away to college, a restless presence at her marriage,

4

waiting for the Higher Cert. results that would confirm his place for dentistry at Newcastle. Two years later, he was a carcase lying on the beach at Dunkirk, and she had resolutely put the image from her, fearful of dislodging Nigel from his queasy resting place in her womb. "We have some native students here from Kenya," Stanley had written to her, and when she had replied in surprise, "Black students?" he wrote back, "No, of course not, Indians to look at but they say they come from East Africa. The black ones come from Nigeria and the Gold Coast and are very contemptuous of European teeth."

She had always remembered that. Why should they need more dentists on the west coast when so many Kenyan teeth were crooked and brown? And who, in other parts of the colony, did the filing and the pulling out that were so obvious? Jack said it was none of her business to ask.

Ellen wondered if Nigel had still kept his boyhood fears, not so much of the dentist as of what happened to his baby teeth. Someone on the farm must have told him he would be in the power of anyone who got hold of his hair clippings or finger nails. (Perhaps it was a well-intentioned warning.) He was always harking back to that, refusing to be comforted. This was something you could hardly ask a grown-up, married man. He had gone off to Australia, where people got lost in the dry desert and were still benighted, by all she heard. His boys would be starting high school now and would never, from what she had seen of them on a visit seven years before, be taught to speak proper English.

The sun was coming out and giving a dry, creepy colour to the bougainvillea, just like the dresses in dull floral patterns they used to wear when she was a girl. In 1930 she had gone to college, fashions sobering down then and the pictures – mostly talkies by that time – giving people big ideas. But in black and white they seemed less extravagant than the glorious technicolour that was to come later. She could recall her mother's horror at the flapper fashions of the 1920s, but she could hardly remember the long dresses of the Great War, only the long faces and the doleful black. She had grown up in short frocks herself and gone to university as though it was her right. They knew they were lucky to have passed the right exams and have enlightened parents who thought girls could be teachers or librarians or even doctors. They did not rightly understand what an extraordinary thing it was to have a father unscathed and a family that could afford to keep you in school beyond the minimum age. School certificate was plenty good enough for going into nursing or office work.

Most of the fatherless had dropped out of sight, claiming that it was more fun to help in a shop or do up the house into furnished apartments. You did know – but not intimately – a few who would spend a year "finishing" in Paris or Geneva, others who would potter around with horses or ceramics or art school until they were swept away into marriage. Bedford College, London, was not in 1930 a very good bet, statistically, for being swept into marriage from. The younger old girls were inclined to say that they valued their freedom. The aunts tended to think it was the men who valued their freedom and did not want to be bossed around. They had not got used to the idea of fairly even numbers. In the generation of the younger aunts, men were in painfully short supply.

They thought this would mean more jobs for women, but many ex-soldiers could be absorbed into teaching with minor disabilities and others took refuge there because they had seen enough of the martial arts to last a lifetime. But they were seldom allowed into segregated girls' schools, and one could be very glad of it. Enormous numbers were out of work. The one-child family for the first time looked normal. A million single women competed for undifferentiated jobs.

Ellen as a student was well aware of privilege, incoherently well-disposed towards the out-of-work and the deprived. Miners were for her the type figures of dispossession. She would have been surprised to learn that many farm labourers were also undernourished or that the girl in the draper's shop was in tatters under her regulation black dress. That knowledge had come to her by later reading when all her assumptions had shifted.

Some girls, even of the kind she had known at school, disappeared into unfamiliar realms, tracing blueprints, demonstrating cookers . . . War widows on small investment incomes were feeling the pinch: even professional men like Ellen's father were running short of clients. Things were swooping side-ways.

Yachts, she remembered, as a detached white cloud bowled along at a spanking pace. Yachts at Cowes, out of one's reach but lovely to watch from the esplanade. Nowadays, her sister Beatrice had written, any Tom, Dick or Harry in Britain could save up enough for a boat if he worked overtime, and the harbours were chock-a-block with them like Oxford gardens with bicycles. Yachts keeling over until one could not imagine how anyone stayed aboard (or had mothers who would let them try). It was all like that, one's expectations toppling at impossible angles and the great European capitals (in which the aunts had been tourists or governesses or ladies' companions) slipping into panic or anarchy with valueless bank notes and a discredited aristocracy. Ellen was sixteen when the last excluded English woman finally got the vote, yet the world of new promise was slithering into a precarious foothold on the deck, where virtue was still demanded without any longer being clearly recognisable.

A bird plunged at a stormy angle overhead: not a sea-bird, of course. Would one see a sea bird again?

In 1934 – September, the beginning of the school year – she started to teach in a Borough Grammar School on the northern edge of London. She lived in a bed-sitting-room which her mother had come with her to seek out. The girls were demure in their uniforms at all times, hair plaited or short bobbed. Perms were announced to be an abomination. Even at the end of the long summer holiday not a trace of one remained. Any girl seen out of doors without her velour brimmed uniform hat would be severely dealt with. Ladies did not go out without a hat. Nor even, in 1934, did women.

The school was new ground for her. Most of the girls had qualified for free places and they were doubly lucky to be allowed to take them up. Parents had to sign a promise to let their daughter stay on till she was sixteen. If they withdrew her, perhaps because the father was injured at work or the mother died, this was considered improvident. Some of the teachers did not seem to see the help the child's small wages could give, or the relief from paying for uniforms, bus fares, sewing materials, hockey sticks. You were supposed to pull the pupil up if the collar of her blouse was scruffy or her hair unwashed. But nobody told you to find out why.

Teachers were still regarded as somebody and got cars quite early on. This was not taken for granted among other professional people, except doctors, of course, who had to do their rounds. Father used to have a little Austin. He let it go about the time Ellen went to university and Stanley was starting at a private boys' day school. They were given to understand that father's eyes were not good enough for driving any more and, of course, medical news was never open to family discussion. That would have been morbid. Mavis had announced, to everyone's dismay, that she knew how to drive, but the offer fell into a pool of silence. What sort of young men could she be cutting around with who would put her at such a risk? (Not to speak of compensation if there were, as seemed inevitable, damage to the vehicle.) The bus service, Mummy remarked brightly, had improved a great deal.

Mavis and Roy soon got engaged and had the use of the grocer's station-wagon outside business hours. Ellen found no problem in travelling alone by bus or underground: people respected teachers, old maids in embryo.

How did it happen then – Miss Mountford into Mrs. Smith? For years she had not dared to think about it. Nobody in Kenya knew Miss Mountford. And, after all, there was no going back. No number of divorces or settlements could make a woman into a girl again or recreate the class idyll in which her perpetually girlish mother had lived. (Ellen was slipping away from corporate life. The name of Margaret Thatcher meant nothing to her. She did not understand how the E.E.C. had superseded Commonwealth preference. But she knew very well that all Beatrice's devices of concealed heating and stereo systems could not give her back Mummy's sublime innocence towards those who served her.)

Ellen had been an easy prey to emotion, which she had perhaps once mistaken for passion. Living in the woman-bound world of a girls' grammar school, hardly meeting a man other than the local librarian or a counterpart from the boys' school, shadowed by her seniors – honest, serious, seldom maudlin – whose actual or potential boyfriends had been killed twenty years before, she could not help being moved by some of Mummy's anxieties about her future. She cared for the girls, cared especially for Lily, since those other few with a feel for the subject and a chance to pursue it beyond school cert were, she thought, more self-sufficient. (Thought so until one of them tried to slash her wrists when her well-off father refused to let her sit for college entrance, but still did not understand the passionate self-reliance of Lily.)

Lily had joined the school in Ellen's second year of teaching. She was a skinny, auburn-haired girl with a sharp Cockney twang to her voice and no sense of reserve. Her self-confidence was absolute, her imagination lively. Her mother, Annie, a green-grocer's assistant well into her forties, retained a spark of her looks and humour. Bert, her father, was proud of her, but himself the grey-faced shadow of a man, gassed in the trenches and seldom able to put in a full week's work.

"Of course he's younger than me," confided Mrs. Beach. "I fancied his older brother, Ernest, but he got himself killed in 1916, so what could I do? My mum said I was a fool to take on a sick man, but a girl's got to get a home of her own, I told her, and they aren't going to go on paying us to make munitions once the war's over. All right for you educated ones, Miss Mountford, and Lily's going to be one of them. Excuse my hands, so red and chapped, that's from being perishing cold all winter washing the veg in cold water for a nice display on the pavement. Well, Lil'll do better than that if I have anything to say about it. Kath, now, she's an usherette in the cinema, not so cushy as you might think, getting home late every night, but she's been ever so good helping me out with Lil's uniform and that. And Walter, not much going for him now. Guess if we had a Hitler Youth here they'd find something for him all right."

10

Lily herself talked ten to the dozen if she happened to meet her favourite teacher on the way to the bus stop.

"At least people are civil to you here. In primary school I got bawled out for not having a penny for a poppy on Remembrance Day. My mum says my dad was gassed in France, isn't that remembrance enough without paying for it? My sister Kath is getting married – well, she has to, you know, but he's the house manager where she works, and what sort of life will that be, Mum says, with him out every evening and you already knowing what sort he is. But a job's a job, isn't it, even with the risks. She couldn't turn it down, and manager's wife is a step up. Mum will miss her twenty-five bob a week coming in. Anyway Mum has taken out a credit cheque, bob a week, to get her some white satin and a bit of blue for me to be bridesmaid. And we can get some flowers from the shop free, and do them up in lace doileys – I'm so excited."

How could you tell her to stop talking until she had achieved a new tone and bearing, found her place within the generally more sober life of the school? Ellen worried a bit about her when she left, but little Lily deluged her with letters. She was evacuated in 1939, so did her school certificate year in the country. Britain had found a niche for her brother Walter by then: his neck was as good a risk as any one else's. Their father was sent to a convalescent home and Mrs. Beach moved down to be near him and did canteen work with the WVS. So, against all expectations, they managed to keep Lily at school through her sixth form, and she got a scholarship to the Old Vic Drama School, doing her first walk-on parts in the New Theatre while desolation reigned round the Waterloo Road.

From there Lily never looked back – controversial actress, white-hot women's libber and, for a time, a toothsome
MP.

*A thread of tinsel or something like it shone in the litter,
perhaps from one of the elaborate greetings cards the
Nakuru old girls liked to send.* Tinsel one used to drape on
Christmas trees or sew on to fairy costumes. There had
been a lot of glitter and silver paper about the school play
where she had, so improbably, met Jack.

It was some scenes from *A Midsummer Night's Dream*
produced with unflagging prettiness by Miss Durrant. Ellen
had helped by hearing the parts. Margaret Ashton made a
handsome Oberon and it was she who had invited Jack, an
older cousin. Whether this was a gesture of haughty confidence on Margaret's part towards the other fifth formers or
an attempt to mask the nervous inadequacies of her own
parents, Ellen did not feel able to judge. Later it appeared
inevitable. Lily had been disqualified for Puck as not correct
enough, though commendably lively.

There was tea afterwards and the staff dutifully circulated among the guests. Jack was feeling awkward, eager
to seize on any face between sixteen and forty. He had come
from Kenya, he explained, to visit his mother, Margaret's
oldest aunt, who was very ill and had now gone into hospital. He was not used to doing for himself in the old house,
so had most of his meals with the Ashtons. He was not sure
whether he would be able to stay to do all that was necessary. The remark dropped like a stone between them. Those
doctors don't tell you much.

He was thirty then, and had gone to Kenya nine years
before, having no chance of getting a job after technical college in that depression time. An uncle on his father's side
had taken up land in the soldier-settler scheme, and had

12

suggested he could make himself useful around the place, at least earn his keep. Crop prices had been poor in Kenya, but the cattle had kept them going: when his own father died he had been able to go into partnership with his uncle, lifting some of the burden of mortgage and taking a half share of the profits. Now the old boy depended on him and it was too bad to take time away. He had thought of buying some farm machinery to take back, but so many people were selling up there that it looked as though it would be better value to buy from them and save the freight. He hadn't, much to do between visiting times, could only take in orange juice for his mother and change the library books, which he wasn't much good at.

Before she knew it, almost, Ellen was charged with changing the library books, brought to the staff-room by Margaret, then with visiting the old lady to find out what she had already read. This involved tea with the Ashtons: the fifth form was buzzing. The expectations of schoolgirls carry weight. Miss Durrant was positively encouraging: it appeared that her brother, dead in Flanders, had a friend who fell victim to blackwater fever as a young District Officer. The memory raised a flutter in her.

Hospital visiting hours were sparse and close-hedged in those days. They would go to one of the new milk-bars afterwards, or for bus rides on Sundays to Kew or Hampton Court. Ellen was flustered. He might not stay long. The staffroom would relapse into whispers, the fifth form into disappointment. At the end of the exam term, the summer holidays loomed. The parents would expect her at Croydon as a matter of course. Mrs. Smith revived sufficiently to justify an occasional visit to a picture-house, Jack's arm tentatively round her, Nelson Eddy and Jeannette Macdonald carolling the sentiments that did not spring easily into words in north London. The Motor Show at Earl's court was the highlight of Jack's visit. Ellen trailed beside him, trying not to spoil his pleasure.

Faltering, she spoke from the tube station to the telephone in Daddy's office. Of course, they would be pleased if she brought a friend over one weekend. Naturally, Jack said, his mother would understand if the Ashtons took over the Sunday visit, two callers only at a time, a strict observance of the bell.

Father and Mother did not seem upset when she suggested going back to her bed-sitter for part of the holidays. There was an exhibition, she said, that would help in preparation for her classes, and Jack's mother (she blushed at the half-truth) expected her to visit. Mrs. Smith, tough old bird, more sharply defined than Mrs. Ashton, had bettered herself, learned in daring Edwardian days to use a typewriter, married the boss's son. Her condition still puzzled the doctors and plagued the nurses, who held death at bay by strict regimen in those times before the wonder drugs. She could not go back to living alone, they said, but might live for years in a convalescent home, if that could be arranged.

"I can't stay," Jack said suddenly. "There's no job for me here and all my money has gone into the farm. In any case, I couldn't ask you to go on nursing her in a house that she will always see as hers, full of dusty china and venetian blinds. But if she would agree to sell the house up – so as to pay for the nursing home, you see – why don't we go back? There will 'be a war here and no end of a mess. Could you make a new start with me? You'd be somebody out there, degree and all that. The girls there grow hard and hefty. I promise you none of them ever took my fancy. You come and see."

14

So there it was. She thought she had made up her mind. Jack was good-looking in a florid, robust way, quiet, cared for his mother, not much of a reader but respected her tastes and opinions: she could not bear to think of him being withdrawn from her. They were sitting on a bench on the Chelsea Embankment. She would miss all this supporting history, but so she might miss it in Sheffield or the Channel Islands.

"Is that really what you want, Jack my dear?" Her tongue could not get round any greater endearment.

"Of course I want it. You know. that."

"Yes, but . . . it is your uncle's house, isn't it? I mean you can't just . . . And can you, I mean the fare and all that? And if you say there will be a war . . ."

He kissed her, though it was still quite light, and so she was quiet. His hands moved more freely after darkness fell. He seemed to know her body better than she did herself: how did he know? But still escorted her chastely home before her landlady could get too worried. He had never thought it proper to invite her to the house.

Mrs. Smith played her gracious part, consented to being sold up (share my home with a schoolteacher, she thought privately, not me and not quite his style either), professed the crowning happiness of getting her son off her hands, produced from somewhere a heavy ring which could be made to fit and saved Ellen the embarrassment of not knowing what she ought to ask for.

"You'll be somebody," Mother said. "Only I wouldn't like you to go on the flying-boat. Nasty things, coming down where all the crocodiles are and creepy jungles, I suppose. Nothing like that where you're going, Jack says. In any case, ships are romantic, a second honeymoon. And space to take all your things for tropical life. Look at Beatrice in India."

Beatrice, five years her elder, was a rather shadowy figure in Ellen's world. Her husband was in customs. It didn't really sound all that exciting, a bungalow on a road with a lot of other English people, mostly more important than you. She had got married at twenty-one the year Ellen was doing her school certificate. Indeed, it was providential that Colin had turned up at that time, having got through his modest ICS exams. Beatrice, like her mother before her, had been a receptionist to their grandfather, Dr. Philip, and he died a few months before the wedding. It was hard to imagine any other job ladylike enough for Beatrice to undertake without any particular training though, on her small salary, she had seemed to the younger ones a very smart young lady. The wedding fell somehow short of expectations — short satin dresses, a low drawn veil for the bride and picture hats for the bridesmaids, sausage rolls, champagne and a two-tier cake in the drawing-room, overflowing into the garden. They saw the happy couple off for a week in Bournemouth, not nearly so exciting as despatching them, a month later, to Southampton to catch the P and O, three weeks tourist class to Bombay: the trousseau dresses had been light and floppy with this in mind. It was not exactly an old Indian family, but one of Colin's uncles had been a military quartermaster and was able to give them a few tips about the way of life.

Mavis, two years older then Ellen, had always been more under her feet than Beatrice, though you could not think of her as a soul-mate. She had been in the same school, finishing ignominiously with four passes and no doubt resenting comparisons with her clever little sister. Mavis was considerately called an outdoor girl, sandy and

16

coarser-skinned than the rest of the family. She would have liked a job in stables but the horse industry was already attracting a higher social stratum. She went to work for a nursery gardener with the hopeful title of florist and spent her wages on cycling and tennis clubs. There she fell in with the son of a small town grocer who had done well and served on the council, and married him in 1932. She had two rollicking little boys and was all in favour of Ellen's "going to see a bit of life. Palm trees, lions, war dances, goings-on in the planter's club, and me still stuck in stuffy Croydon." She looked happy enough.

"But the climate," Mummy persisted. Beatrice and the babies had looked so peaky that one time they came on leave. And the expense of having to go away in the hot weather. It was clear to Ellen that they seldom managed it. Jack said it was not too hot round Nakuru, the Njoro side. You could stay for years without a break. (He could say that again!) Of course you had to have a car because of the distance, no problem, and feel you were building up a country and making a better life for people. The workers on the farm learned a lot.

"If she gets bored with the farm," he went on, "there are schools in Nakuru she can teach in."

"But married ladies don't teach." (In the years of unemployment they were not allowed to, even if they had no children of their own.)

"And you say it is a small town. You don't just teach anything. The vacancies might not be suitable."

"Well, it isn't quite the same, you know. People from all round have to go into town to school – some of them are boarders. All sorts. But I'm not saying you have to do it. Only if you get bored, with someone else to do the housework, you see. And I know you're not really an outdoor type."

"But housekeeping is a lot more than house-work," put in Mummy bravely.

"If Chamberlain doesn't pull us out of it, we'll all be doing things we never expected." Daddy looked as though he meant it. Stanley, immersed in Higher Cert Biology, offered his views on reproduction in farm animals.

"Now there is no need to be coarse, dear. And I daresay you will be spending a vacation with them one of these days, and finding out how much more Jack knows about it than you do."

Daddy was tight-lipped after discussing the financial position with Jack, but committed himself to the statement that on a farm you cannot go short of essentials. (He had never seen a swarm of locusts, and had fixed ideas about education and medical insurance.) He would be happy to deal with the elder Mrs. Smith's financial affairs as a family matter, and this took a weight off Jack's mind.

Passages were booked, with a little flutter over the names. Ellen had got a passport already, having helped to take a school party to France the year before. She gave in her notice. Jack persuaded her that his uncle would be perfectly happy to divide the house and no new furniture would be necessary. (He could say that again!) He insisted on her taking driving lessons.

Beatrice wrote from India with advice about managing the servants and the hot weather. She expressed pleasure that Ellen would have a wider horizon and a more comfortable life.

Wider? Comfortable? Ellen did not claim to know the world but she knew her Kipling and her Forster. And from chinks between Jack's determinedly cheery sentences she was getting a picture of Kenya. Pioneers going deaf from too much quinine among the worthless coffee trees. Veterinary officers ploughing through the mud. Leopards, ticks, locusts, jiggers, public schoolboys writing down hearty, cliche-ridden speeches to be read on Empire Day, while native police sweated in their jumpers and tarbooshes. Black people all round, respectful but not very far on the road to uplift, breathing a risk of typhoid and sleeping sickness. Peers of the realm shooting at lamp standards. Missionary battle axes demanding a special price on mosquito nets. Goan Catholics in the clerical services. Black clergy giving Holy Communion to their flock. The obsequious Indians of the bazaar creeping in to the professions, even into politics: she did not yet know that they would sleep in the same college hall as Stanley, but they could not be hereditary rulers as in India. Even Beatrice would be civil to a Rajah's son.

The wedding in October was not a climax but a preliminary to sailing. Mavis was Matron of Honour. Margaret Ashton had to be bridesmaid. Ellen would have liked to bring some of the other girls from school, but it would have been embarrassing to invite Lily to a middle-class home so she did not ask any of them. She wore a white two-piece and a big tropical hat. The wedding presents had to be packed immediately – Mavis was good at this – while they spent a few days at a quiet hotel in London, visiting Jack's mother and taking leave of history. East Africa must have a history but it had not yet been brought to their notice. People had no idea that their earliest ancestors had roamed among the tropical lakes. Maps homed in on the railway. Nakuru looked a terribly long way from the proper sea.

Of course it would be all right, but... Mother hustled them as though only Europe could have a war. They took the boat, tourist class, hobnobbing with housekeepers and policemen, celibatè in shared cabins, yet feeling privileged in the adventure. Over the glare on the water, strident voices made her sense already what was to come – the subtle grading of white society, even in the church, the covert presence of the other races. Farm wives with coarse hands and coarse talk revealing the sheer hard grind of their lives and missionary teachers swapping methods and boning up on languages. In Kenya there were lords all over the place but, someone dared to say, no ladies.

Mr. Mountford would not have been surprised: in blessing the precarious move to Africa he was more realistic than the rest of the family about what a war might mean. Lawyers, even in the Home Counties where people keep up appearances, learn about heartbreak and financial loss, unmentionable injuries, hidden scandals and thwarted affections. The world was going to the dogs in his opinion. The king's abdication two years before typified the signs of the times. For one client Mr. Mountford had arranged the adoption of orphaned Jewish children from Germany. Even when the sort of thing that happened to their parents was reported in the British press people did not seem able to take it in. Still less did they believe it could happen here. The Empire, he thought, might hold out longer than the old country, even with less spit and polish.

Chapter 2

Mrs. Smith was fast asleep now, breathing noisily, her head rolling across the cushions, her hands clutching a handkerchief. Martha tucked the cardigan over her arms and brushed the crumbs onto the grass for the birds to deal with. It was not work, really, just what had to be done. Everything around her was familiar.

She had managed to institute tea without a traycloth when there were no visitors. For a fortnight Mrs.Smith had not raised the question. It was not that a servant need have opinions about unnecessary washing: it is so often the unnecessary that one gets paid for. Mrs. Smith would have to acknowledge that herself if she had occasion to listen to some of the extravagant English her former pupils used to one another in the amusement arcades after all the loving care and oral exercises she had lavished upon them. But these days the constant trembling of the tea-cup, misplacement of spoon, crumbling of eatables, reduced the life of a clean cloth to minutes or seconds, and the wear and tear was terrible, considering how old they were already. One had to be practical.

The housework she knew in her bones, learned of her father, not her mother, for father had worked in a European house in Nakuru and brought her when she was quite small to stay with him and go to school, while mother weeded at home and carried the waterdrums on her bent back. Her childhood seemed to have been spent mouselike in kitchens, watching him scrub tables and wield the heavy charcoal iron. She completed standard four and then went back to help her mother, laughed at for her prissy ways and straight back, until the time came to be married. Martha's mother had always been cynical about the unnecessary

fiddle-faddles of the European, on which her husband ex-
peded his working life. Yet their own. home had then
seemed well-equipped. Never a margarine-tin was thrown
away where her father worked without being transformed
into a mug, a miniature oil-lamp or a flour sifter. Her
mother's generation had not applied the same prudence to
the conservation of energy.

*She carried a stool out and sat close to the old lady,
sipping her own tea and staying her hand from wiping away
the wet rings on the glass-topped tray.* You could not always
clear away the mess or preserve the eager cleanness of your
heart. She had known a young teacher who used to sleep
hitched to the branch of a tree to avoid the Mau Mau oath
administrator, but of course it was no good. They got him
down and threatened to torture his wife and children if he
did not assent.

A fan-shaped plant with red berries had been planted
along the fence. Not quite holly, that you had pictures of at
Christmas time, but Mrs. Smith used to say that holly, even
on the bush, never seemed quite real to her, the glazed
leaves improbably curved like something made of plastic,
the prickles less than naturally sharp.

The holly bears a berry

as red as any blood,

like the Sacred Heart the Roman Catholics pictured, the
hard, stylised drops of blood, terribly extracted from the
Christian Kikuyu as they had been from those other guerilla fighters in the heathlands of Europe, so her son-in-law
had told her. Surely Jesus' blood was not like that, not mea-
sured out in drops but free-flowing.

Ellen stirred and reached out to a ray of sunlight. First
arrival at Mombasa had come close to her picture-book

22

anticipation of Africa, but Jack's conversation hinged on a series.of negatives:

"Of course in Nakuru it is not like this . . . people are properly dressed ... there are more Europeans . . . the food keeps better."

They spent one night in the Palace Hotel, the bare, mosquito-curtained bed a refuge from the need to explore the narrow streets of the old town or the ferry in the all-absorbing heat. To lie together had not become a habit: there was no need to spend out on a first class compartment for two in the train next evening. Ellen shared its queer, rattling progress with three older ladies who were known to one another and conversed like schoolteachers of a small, closed world, throwing out an occasional explanatory sent-ence in her direction. She was content to watch the palm trees and the village where smiling children waved, inter-spersed with tracts of bush and thorn trees, until the blinds were firmly drawn by her companions, unenchanted with the African night, and they disposed themselves to sleep, showing her how to hoist the ladder to the top bunk.

Mrs. Smith continued to doze, and Martha wheeled her up the ramp on to the verandah, bumping the chair as little as she could. There was a lot to do on the days visitors were expected, if Martha was to keep up the standards she expected of herself. But it made a change to have someone else take an interest in Mrs. Smith and judge how she was getting on. Yourself, seeing her daily and occupied with your own aches and pains, you might miss something significant.

Ellen woke as the click and slide of the wheels began again after one of the interminable stops. Blinds were still drawn, so she managed to clamber down and open the door into the corridor so that she could watch colour creep into the sky and enlighten the endless, indistinguishable

23

scrubland. The view was constantly interrupted by khaki-clad figures carrying bedding-rolls, passengers making for the toilets, fathers searching for wives and children in the ladies' compartments and waiters holding trays of tea silent against the lurching of the train.

"It would be better," enunciated a single voice, speaking for the three ladies, "to let one know when unbolting the door. Thefts have been known to occur." The voice indicated worse than theft.

"I was just outside," Ellen replied. "No one could have come in without my knowing."

"Aaah!" The inhabitant of the other top bunk was already dressed and corsetted. "You have no idea how quick they can be. We had already made a rota for the wash-basin inside. It is not necessary to visit the cloakroom until . . ." A hand deprecated her neat cotton wrapper. Fortunately Jack strolled along and saved her having to give an acid reply. She excused herself, dressed in the toilet and went along to his compartment for the rest of the trip.

"Newly married," she heard spat out as the door slid to behind her. "Admittedly everybody has to use the same train, but there is a certain standard to keep up."

The train brought them in the early morning through the African part of the town – small rows of small quarters interspersed with wattle and daub or tin shanties. Here and there a school or police post was fenced off with trim grass and paths. Goats, chickens, patches of maize and vege-tables, children waving, women already setting out washing amazingly white on dusty bushes, lines of men trudging to work. It didn't look big enough to contain all the workaday needs of a big town: well, perhaps it was only one of many quarters, she reasoned, and could not ask questions as Jack introduced his travelling companions and the luggage was ranged in order.

Outside the station they took a taxi to the Ainsworth Hotel, eight shillings a day and within walking distance of the town. So this was Nairobi, a name to conjure with, a jumble of other people's impressions now confronting the reality – the earnest geography teacher mumbling about quinine and watersheds – people on the boat planning theatricals and nature walks – the ladies on the train disdainful of commerce and fortune-hunters – a teacher in Mombasa who had explained that these days anything might happen and you had better keep yourself to yourself – Jack who said it was just like outer London really, so long as you kept your sun-glasses on.

After breakfast and a bath (there was also a tumble on the bed but she suppressed the memory of that) he took her out to show her that there was everything essential to a town. She had to agree: there were churches, mosques, a town hall, Memorial Hall where the Legislative Council sat, tea-shops, motor showrooms, department stores (two), war memorials, picture postcards, a daily newspaper . . . Perhaps it was more like a market town servicing the region outside than a city, but the neat rows of bungalows for European railway workers by the station reminded you that people also lived here. More adequate than the labour lines but conceived in the same spirit, they threatened a glimpse of Beatrice's life in India.

Of the impressions, Jack's were (properly and reassuringly) the nearest to being right. Contrasts – without the sun-glasses – were sharper than she was used to – brilliant flowers, barefoot porters, hennaed hands, glittering saris, brown wrinkled European faces, family grocers nestling among the three - or four-storey office buildings.

There were still rickshaws stationed in Duke Street but cars and bicycles predominated. Their taxi driver was a Somali (Jack said) and very polite. White people or English-speaking Indians served you in the big city shops: of course in the country it would be different. Just as at home, some had cars, some used buses, some pushed barrows, and at home, too, you were cut off in an undefined way from the stall-holders or the office cleaners. People like Lily and the taxi driver moved across the divide.

It was November, the short rains in abeyance for a few days. Nobody mentioned the black glutinous mud which often sucked at the station end of the town. Shops were already displaying things for Christmas, incongruous to Ellen under a blue sky. No, not too early, the lady in the hotel explained. The seasonal surface mail had already gone for overseas and people from upcountry would want to do their shopping in one big bust when they came in. So *Beano Annual* was already in the shops, *The Nipper* and *Rupert* of the *Daily Express*. There were coloured lights and one or two windows showed cotton wool or artificial holly, pathetic brightener of the winter solstice, dingy against the splendour of the flowering trees.

Next afternoon they picked up their heavy luggage at the station and arranged themselves on the train ready for home-coming. The railway ran right through town, bisecting Delamere Avenue and passing the Scottish Church on its way up to Chiromo, where the first non-official whites had pitched their tents, and flourishing Westlands.

"That's as near to Croydon as we come," said Jack. Ellen put on her neatest blouse and tried to remember whether she had ever actually been on a farm – only the sort that put on strawberry teas for summer visitors or demonstrated a model dairy to schoolgirls. She guessed how

26

much her future depended on getting along with Uncle, but the domestic prospect was still blank to her. Was it that she had never asked the necessary questions, or had Jack avoided answering them? Could you move into a house without knowing what you would use to cook on or how far away the chickens were?

"Sorry we're not very much in the clear for shopping," said Jack ruefully, "but I suppose you don't know what you'll need until you've seen the place. Anyway, we've managed to keep going up to now. If there's anything urgent you can be sure to get it in Nakuru – provided Uncle has been keeping everything under control. I telegraphed him to meet us, of course. He can't wait to set eyes on you."

Uncle did indeed meet them in the middle of the night off the train with an ancient Ford, a smacking kiss for Ellen and a wink at Jack.

"Done yourself a bit of all right, eh? We've been needing a woman about the place for years, my dear. Didn't reckon on getting a lady into the bargain. But you'll transform the house – isn't that right, Jack? Transform it, and that's an invitation. I have my corner and my papers and my baccy. Beyond that it's all yours, and welcome."

She knew at once that he meant it. High coloured face, a bit stubbly, shrunken under loose skin, old flannels and a knitted cardigan redolent of pipe tobacco, eyes rejuvenated after just a few beers.

"Had myself a day in the town, Jack, to celebrate. Went to a sale at old Mick's but not much worth picking up there. Lovely Jersey calf we got off Buttercup, called her Ellen in honour of your missus. Good that Chamberlain got us a breather at Munich, peace for the moment, whether with honour or not I wouldn't like to have to say. Otherwise I was afraid you'd both be stuck there winning the war. I didn't fancy that, Ellen, didn't like the sound of it at all.

"Look here, that trunk's more than these springs'll stand for. We'll get someone to look after it, pick it up next trip. I don't suppose you've left y'r diamond tiara in there, have you? You sit in the front, girl, while we just get that luggage stowed."

They cruised through the lighted streets, Jack driving. It was not quite like a miniature Nairobi, though her impressions, like her surroundings, were shadowed. Steps up to high pavements, shops set under verandahs, dust and wooden shutters.

"Hold on to your hat, now."

And he meant it. A neat blue felt, close to the head. They lurched off on to a rougher road: she braced her knees and thought it was better than she expected. By the time she had got used to the rhythm they lurched again, and this time it was worse than she had ever dreamed of.

"Getting near home now. Private property, practically speaking."

She kept bumping into Jack as the ruts threw her up and down. It was pitch black outside, noisy with crickets and the howl of a distant dog. "Home sweet home," Uncle called, and a figure moved to open the gate. On the wooden verandah someone in white threw open a door and set out lanterns. The very same verandah, looking almost as it did today. Atlas Wood Preservative had lived up to its pre-war advertisements.

"I told Kirui he needn't stay up, but the sense of occasion overwhelmed him," said Uncle.

Jack put down a suitcase and propelled her up the steps. Perhaps in the sudden light he had noticed how pale and shaky she was.

The servant, a green cummerbund belting his long *kanzu*, was bowing and smiling, picking up luggage, ushering her into a big shabby sitting-room where insects swirled around the pressure-lamp and a tray of drinks, tea in a thermos, scones under a paper napkin were spread out.

"Lovely. Home. Thank you," she acknowledged to all of them, "*Asante, mzuri,*" grasping at language lessons on the boat.

"You did say for better or worse," grinned Jack.

"So we both did." She wanted to say "This is for better," but was not sure it actually came out; her knees were giving way and she half fell into a chair. Would they believe the tears were simply due to exhaustion? Uncle held up a tea-cup and she nodded. He filled it and put it with sugar on the stool beside her.

"Well, good night, good night: take you on a tour tomorrow – afternoon, say. Morning for sleeping. High altitude makes you tired."

He was gone. Kirui ceremonially closed the front door and retreated to the kitchen. Jack gave her a hand to the bathroom – roomy, old-fashioned, basin, fitted bath, flush toilet with a chain: goodness knows where the water came from, but she had been prepared for a zinc tub and a box seat. The twin beds were made up, towels laid out, windows fastened, boiled water in a bottle for cleaning teeth. Jack's arm firmly round her as she lay in a stupor. Home.

Intermittently she was conscious of cocks crowing, gates clashing, small birds twittering: all the time she could feel the slow shudder of the train, the jolting of the old car on the rutted track, a layer of dust dimming her perception. When she awoke, Jack was gone and the sun burst upon her as she opened the faded, flowered curtains. She put on a housecoat to go to the bathroom and found Kirui fussing on the verandah.

"Tea, memsahib? Coffee? Toast? Bacon? Eggs?"

She knew it would not do to go to the kitchen herself. Not just yet.

"Some tea, please, Kirui, and bread and butter: perhaps a boiled egg. Sorry I slept late. You also waited up for us."

"Very happy, Mrs. Smith."

She spent the morning touching things, marking out a territory. The men clattered in to a heavy lunch — stew, mounds of potatoes, hunks of pineapple.

"Well, got over the worst?" grinned Jack.

"Very happy. Sorry about last night. It was as though something knocked me out."

"Everything strange," said Uncle placidly. "Take your time. Should have seen him when he first came. Thought milk was made in a bottle and grass was something to play cricket on. Still, he's learned a bit since then, I do say. Now he knows which way is up." So they did the rounds. To the pasture first, wisely, where the little calf won her heart, to the maize field, the oat field, the vegetable garden, the dairy, the barn. To meet Musa the clerk, Njoroge the headman, Kimalel the cattle man, Njoki weeding the second crop maize, Kamau cutting back the encroaching hedges which a younger Uncle had unwisely preferred to fencing, Njoroge's son, Sam, looking after the chickens, Kimalel's son Felix checking over the tractor, old Mwangi sunning himself before taking over the night watch.

30

She thought she would never remember them all, never be able to distinguish the kinds of grass and cereals. As a compromise she started by learning the kinds of cows. What they told her about acreages and yields and prices passed her by. They saved for another day the little conical huts that housed the staff. It all tied in, of course, with what Jack had told her, but she had only managed to visualise it in a much smaller scale. Clearly it could be lived in. How a living could be made on it was another matter and beyond her.

She wrote to tell her mother, Beatrice, Mavis, her school head, her art teacher friend, what the farm was like and how you could frame your life within it. There were long hours for writing when she would have been washing and ironing if Kirui would let her, marking compositions if there were a way to bring her two worlds together, planting flowers if she had known how to match them with soil and shade. She practised driving over the ruttled lane, found out what things cost so that she could plan the menu, tried her hand at baking on the old wood range, mastered the art of lighting the pressure lamp, hurricane lamp, primus stove.

She learned a few Swahili sentences into which she could fit some of the words she had memorised on the boat, and observed the different pitch and tempo of the Kikuyu language which most of the workers used among themselves. Ignorance oppressed her. She had listened attentively to the missionaries' advice in those simple Swahili lessons on deck. "Do not count children, always offer with the right hand, start every enquiry with a greeting." But nobody had told her that one language would not be enough. The rising inflection heard in the *duka* battered on her ears: unfamiliar vowels and aspirates bewildered her. People expected

31

her to code instructions, not to converse, least of all to over-hear.

Even when the standard Swahili dictionaries were published next year and she hastened to buy them, she was not much the wiser, since they started so many words in the middle.

"Dictionary," scoffed Jack, "for that lingo? And you're supposed to be the clever one. *I* never have any trouble making myself understood."

But how much of Jack did anyone understand?

Much of normal life seemed to be suspended. At the end of the month, Uncle pressed three hundred shillings in small notes into her hand: "That's for my keep," he said. She did not know how to respond. This would keep him for a month at the Ainsworth Hotel. But it became apparent that it was keep for all the three of them. Prices were absurdly low for produce, high compared with England for manufactured goods, she thought, exploring Nakuru one day when the neighbourly Galsworthys had offered a lift. She bought flour, cooking fat, fruit, was puzzled by the fish and decided to leave it. Christmas was coming but she must be cautious: cake fruit and fancy paper seemed expensive. She had five English pounds left to change at face value in the bank. Jack paid Kirui, she supposed, and eggs, chickens, milk, cabbage and beans came free from the farm. Prices were so low it was hardly worth selling them anyway. Butter and cheese could be bought from the Holmeses, beer and cigarettes from a store on one of the larger farms. There was no refrigerator so meat had to be salted or smoked if you bought a side of beef when someone was slaughtering. Kirui showed her how to do it. That gave her an opening to extend his range of salads and puddings.

There was a big wooden-floored sitting-room joined by the verandah to the three bedrooms, each with a fireplace for the cold weather and mosquito netting: the corrugated iron roof was hidden by hardboard ceilings over which you heard occasional bumps and scampering. The kitchen and bathroom were at the far side, entered by doors at each end of the verandah. Back steps went down to ground level from the kitchen, with a yard for laundry and space wired off for the hens to peck about. Water-taps and cistern were fed from the outside tank – in dry seasons you had to be a bit careful, they told her. The bathroom and kitchen floors were cemented because of the water but the board floor, varnished but hardly worth polishing, seemed more homely in the big bedroom which she shared with Jack. She still felt like a visitor there.

The furniture was locally made of wood, dark-stained with flock cushions covered in flowered cotton – nothing you could object to, nothing you would have chosen. She had brought out her wedding china and linen and a few water-colours done by a friend who used to teach art. These lightened the air a little. She asked advice at the seed shop and planted flowers round the three sides of the house skirted by the verandah. Direct sunlight did not penetrate indoors and one never quite got away from the smell of chickens and woodsmoke. She was glad that the house was only fifty yards away from the track they referred to as the road, so that the rest of the farm paraphernalia lay behind them.

The farm was foreign ground, though she tried to learn what had to be done when Jack was away. Njoroge would creak on to the verandah to report absentees or stock deaths. Jack had frozen her with a look the first time she offered him tea. Now it was understood the cook could give him something at the kitchen door.

Payout was done down at the store the last Saturday of the month. Jack would be called if there was a difficult calving or a hen pecking her eggs. At first he would show her these things, but seemed to take no pleasure in his special knowledge. Barring emergencies, this was none of her business. Those reporting sick could be taken into town on Saturdays. She had not yet dared face up to them with iodine and epsom salts, but she sometimes accompanied the clinic run and struck up an acquaintance with Sister O'Brien. Confinements did not seem to get any help at all. One time she had given a lift from the junction to a woman carrying a new-born who was not breathing properly: it died before they got to the hospital. Ellen insisted on taking the mother to the clinic but did not stay to watch what happened. She was terrified: in her experience babies, once normally delivered, did not die. She had no concept of what formalities and interrogation might follow. She had no language in common with the mother and could not find out what farm she lived on.

"Probably walked straight home again," said Jack when she told him in the evening. "Tough as old boots, these bints."

She never mentioned such an incident to him again.

Uncle now and again roused himself to enthusiasm – "Lovely breeding cow, that Guernsey cross: never gave us any trouble since the day she was born" – and he noticed when she polished up the brass jug to put flowers in. He had a sweet tooth: "Never used to have hot puddings like this before you came," he would say clumsily. "Good thing for us Jack set eyes on you, though I dessay he had other things in mind than fritters and spotted dick." If Jack had, he didn't see much need to refer to them.

A couple of miles down the track you turned into a road that at least attempted drainage and a pedestrian edge: three miles from that brought you to the main Nakuru road which the map described as "all-weather", as though the paths and lanes could opt out of any kind of weather if they chose. This was where buses and lorries passed daily, heading west to Kisumu or east to Nairobi, perhaps even Mombasa. Here marched the telephone lines, and in Nakuru there was electric light. One or two hotels and the biggest farms had their own generators, but this was not a realistic object of ambition. Lamplight and crude water arrangements she had foreseen: it was this never-ending gritty distance of things that she could not get used to, not having libraries, corner grocers, or near neighbours.

On Bonfire Night or Empire Day you were expected to trek into the Club. You could drive to church for the English service, taken by a white chaplain, while your staff had their own, livelier-sounding worship in quarters or out of doors. The ordained, black padre would occasionally attend, puffing up on his bicycle. Once the cowman came to ask her for a slice of bread for Holy Communion: she had given him half a loaf and asked what they would do for wine. The padre would bring it in his saddle-bag, she was told. There were some new communicants who had been confirmed the last time the Bishop came to Nakuru. Mr. Holmes had let them use his pick-up, provided they put petrol in, to attend the service. How was it she had not known? A secret life was going on round her, another thing she had not anticipated. Perhaps the missionaries could explain it to her, but the nearest missionaries, as far as she knew, were those who had the industrial school at Londiani. White children could get Sunday school lessons by correspondence, but what about the others, who did not know how to read or, if they did, had no money for pencils and stamps?

"You don't want to encourage that kind of caper," the other farmers said. "If you get them all legally married, two by two, there won't be enough women to work in season: they are cheaper than the men. And if you start schools, the children will go away to the towns to be clerks. Better leave them as they are."

So where did the clerks come from in towns, the school messenger, the shop assistants, the railways attendants?

"From the reserves," said the farmers, "Where these Africans do so well on their *shambas* that we have to have quotas to restrict what they can sell. There they have plenty of money for school fees, and after school their sons go out and get good wages and bicycles and shoes . . .

"All very well for you," they said, "going to be teaching these *dukawallahs* I suppose, you would be bored just living on a farm, you with a degree and all that" (red envy in their eyes)– "but just don't get them on too far, educating them to take our jobs and our land. They are getting a stranglehold over us already . . ."

(It was true in a way: Uncle explained that many of them would not have survived without Indian credit for wire netting and liquor, or without laws to restrict what the Indians could take as security.)

The neighbours were kind, if a bit wary: ladies drove their milk trucks out of their way, off the Nakuru road, to introduce themselves and welcome the newcomer, dropping hints from the *Kenya Settlers' Cookery Book* or first-hand tips about poultry breeding and cockroach repellent. Some invited them over for drinks or supper, sending over a note by a farmhand or catching Jack at a sale to issue the invitation. One Sunday they were asked out to Mrs. Grant's and drove there in their best clothes.

"You would have got on well with Elspeth, dear, but she is away again, you have just missed her," announced Nellie Grant, and Ellen realised that at least she was safe with her name: the diminutive was already appropriated. Mrs. Grant was bouncing with ideas as usual – breeding exotic birds, introducing her staff to Scottish dancing, weaving with noisy machines in a tin shed . . . Jos Grant showed them amiably round: "No money in mixed farming," he announced, "but it keeps her cheerful till I can get something really worthwhile going." He was happier than Mr. Micawber in that others carried on making a living regardless of his schemes.

"It takes all kinds to make a world, dear," Mrs. Grant assured Ellen, "even a little inward-looking world like ours. So don't let them tie you down to knitting patterns and charity bazaars if you don't like it. You'll be good at languages, I expect? Too many of us have been lazy about that and missed so much about the people around us. You know I went to stay with Elspeth in the reserve near Karatina when she was getting ready to write *Red Strangers*, and I'm glad I did, never mind who's looking down her nose. I might have missed all the fun I've had in Kenya if it hadn't been for the Crash at home, but at least I had a family I needn't be ashamed of talking about. Some of these, putting on airs like Lady Muck . . . Well, I need to remember the three monkeys. We can speak no evil even if it's pretty hard to see no evil among our high and mighty neighbours. Anyway you can teach, of course, once you've settled down a bit. And I can see you're going to bring out the best in Jack. Just look on the bright side."

Ellen nodded. It would be more comfortable to know that Jack was going to bring out the best in her.

"Uncle has been marvellous," she ventured.

"Old Smithie? One of nature's gentlemen. You'll be the light of his eyes soon."

"I am really not all that keen on going back to teaching."

"I can understand that, but you'll need something. They are eager to learn, too. Even the whites. On the farms some haven't had much grounding, you see. But think it over. You need something for yourself."

But teaching was not getting something for yourself, it was the strength constantly draining out of you. A letter from Lily reminded her of it: "We did all right in the exams, Miss – Mrs. Smith, I ought to say – but things are duller without you. Of course we are glad you got married and all that. I hope you don't find that grass and cows too boring. Miss Austin says there are not likely to be any lions left your way but I would be looking out for a lion or two if I was, were (I mean) you."

December slipped by. She bought, shame-faced at the meanness of it, a diary for Jack, a cartoon annual for Uncle, a bag of sweets for the children on the farm, some shampoo and hairslides for herself, since the perm she had had for the wedding was growing out and, though there was a hairdresser in Nakuru, she did not think she ought to spend out: in any case there was not much high fashion around the farms.

You could fill out your mincemeat with plums, the ladies told her. Plums? At Christmas time? Yes, certainly. They will be coming into the market any day now. You can have a cold pudding or a plum duff. (Throw a few raisins in for the colour.) Chickens for the asking. Leave Jack to look after the drinks: he's an expert. We'll give you a lift into church if he's not going. See you at the party at the club.

Three-year-old dresses. Paper hats. Pancake make-up or none (the perspiration, you see). Men in thin jackets, like waiters. One red wine, thank you. No, she didn't care for gin. (Actually had never tasted it.) Dancing to the gramophone. Jack, red-faced, repeating some of the stories he had heard on the boat.

"Made a square deal with Jerry at Munich," someone was saying, "but if he plays up again we'll trounce him same as last time."

"If we had our king he would have talked them round," put in a fruity voice. "Good time we had when the Prince of Wales came, you remember, Ted? This one not bred for the job. Wouldn't say boo to a goose."

"Don't agree with you there, old man. Put his hand to the plough, won't turn back."

"Bloody aristocracy married all over Europe."

"Hardly for us to criticise, old boy. Bloody aristocracy married or not married all over Kenya, I'd say. Not all of 'm'll be running back home if there's a call to arms."

"You will be Mrs. Smith, I take it? . . . Too much to expect these fellows to make a formal introduction, so excuse me... I've been keeping an eye on you from a distance, so to speak. I'm the Education Officer . . ."

"Oh dear, don't say you are going to nag me again about teaching."

"Well, I wouldn't want to *nag*, of course, but we are a bit desperate for trained people. We don't have secondary here yet, and the European school is fully staffed, but the Asian boys' primary really needs strengthening. As soon as Mr. Smith told me . . ."

"But I'm only just *married*, didn't he tell you that? I had no thought of going back to work. And I'm not trained for primary. I wouldn't know where to start. It's not fair on them . . ."

"Of course you must take your time to think it over. But many of our wives get bored at home, you know, having someone to help them with the housework and not a lot of relations around. In fact, while the locusts and the low produce prices were hitting us, we had the most unsuitable people offering – you wouldn't believe, some we really could not . . . Well, this is not the place to talk about it. But you must see that the parents appreciate, the boys are keen, if we could get to a certain level we would be eager to have the girls . . . Please do think about it. I won't go into terms now but really they are not too bad."

What could she do but promise to think it over? But with a sinking of the heart. Did these people realise you were supposed to be getting pregnant? Were you meant to plan your time, like your trousseau, without considering the possibility? All this starting and stopping did not look to her like professional competence. Why assume you could only pull your weight by making money? She would not have enjoyed the club in any case, so it was not just this conversation that spoiled the Christmas party. But this club was the best she was being offered. "Many of our wives . . ." Good grief!

She had it out with Jack that night, though he was not at his most lucid.

"I told you you would be bored at home. People don't make a bomb out of bottling lemon curd and pickle, even if you were inclined that way. For heaven's sake what's wrong with taking a job for a while? Yes, of course I'd like children, but let's face that when it comes, or put it off a bit if you like. Christ! I never told you the farm was a moneyspinner, did I? Four and a half months I was away, wedding suit, week in Kensington, your passage back and all that. Now you want to look a gift horse in the mouth? Anything you can do to help on the farm Musa can do better for fifty shillings a month and glad of it. My goodness, Mrs. Grant went off to England for three months and left Muchoka to look after things. I don't say I'd go that far in the way of brotherly love myself, but anyone who's got a job in prospect might as well take it before any De Sousa, Mwangi or Patel comes to shove him out of the way."

He was soon snoring and she cried herself to sleep. Next time he was out for the day she tackled Uncle at lunchtime.

"You know they want me to go and teach? I feel I've hardly settled yet. How can I face it?"

He looked at her blankly.

"Of course we don't have to hurry you, but you'll find it hard to sit here and twiddle your thumbs all day. Besides, a bit of pocket money, some new dresses, a holiday at the coast, maybe. Times are better than they have been but the farm doesn't run to much of that, you see. Mortgage to pay off. I understood Jack talked to your dad about it.

"We never had any kids, you know. Emily used to get bored so she'd scrub the paint off almost before it was dry for want of something to do. (Wouldn't have an inside servant, Emily. Just one to bring the water and chop the wood and kill the chickens for her.) She died before Jack came to stay with me. Living on her nerves, that's what. You make up your own mind, of course. But if I were you, I'd take that job."

Christmas passed in a haze of wood smoke, alcohol and the goat they had given the staff to roast in the quarters. The church service was hot and unmoving. Uncle had somehow obtained and secreted till Christmas morning a bunch of roses and fern for her. Jack came up with a box of chocolates. Christmas cards hung on a string above the fireplace. The next working day she begged for use of the car and went to the Education Office.

"Lunch, madam," Martha shrilled in Mrs. Smith's ear. (Really Martha was becoming quite noisy nowadays as though one were not paying attention.) *Mince meat, mashed potatoes, peas, carrots, fruit salad, all quite easy to manage.* Martha must have ducked back into the kitchen to eat hers. She had learned to bolt it , no doubt, so as to be ready for the next chore – some employers had no consideration. All the same, not like the manners Mummy had been so fussy about when she was still hoping to make a lady of you.

"You remember Mrs. Banerjee is coming this afternoon," Martha reminded her. *"So we'll wait for the tea, shall we? Why don't you get changed and finish with the bathroom? Then I can get you settled in the shade before she comes . . . Yes, I know you can manage, but it would help me to get ahead. The spotted dress?"*

When all had been manoeuvred, Martha pushed the wheel-chair down the ramp again and over to the shade of the pepper-tree, and set the stool with a bell, a woollie, some magazines, beside it. Then she locked the wheels with a little click.

There had been just such a click of the door as she now heard, a tentative jangling, as of the bell being set down, when the Education Officer took her that first time round to see Mr. Patel (R.J. Patel, she learned later) the chairman of the primary school board. The pleasure on Mr. Patel's face

42

was the most heartening part of the whole transaction. He insisted that she choose herself a present from the shop to celebrate the bargain, and she chose a fine wool scarf in cream and pink, reverently wrapped up by the girl behind the counter.

"This is Niranjana," said Mr. Patel proudly. "We taught her to read and write at home. Perhaps because of you the younger ones will have a better chance."

Chapter 3

*A car was coming in the gate. Martha must have unlocked it
in the morning. One of the young men from the cooperative
farm sprang to open it for Mrs. Banerjee in her neat little
Fiat. (In those old days you would never have got a Fiat
over the ruts even if Mr. Smith and Mr. Banerjee would
have countenanced the visit.) Mrs. Smith could not see
which young man, but really they were very kind to old
ladies. Of course, some of them had been born here.*

*Mrs. Banerjee waved and took her time about parking
the car. She was nerving herself to face her old colleague.
Her hair was quite white now but beautifully waved, and
she walked a bit stiffly. Perhaps she had never walked all
that much. She was sensibly dressed in a neat, dark sari
with a white cardigan over the blouse. She took Mrs. Smith's
hand in both of hers.*

*"How are you, my dear? You look much better today.
And what lovely weather!" Mrs Smith expressed her pleasure in an unintelligible mumble. Mrs. Banerjee greeted
Martha who had come on to the verandah in a clean, flowered dress. She would be needed as interpreter. This was
understood. On the pretext of handing over her basket of
home-made savouries, Mrs. Banerjee followed her back to
the kitchen.*

*"How is she, Martha? I know it is hard work for you. Do
you think she should have a nurse? Is there any way I can
help?"*

*She had started to speak in her limited Swahili, then
hastily changed to English, recognising Martha as part of a
sisterhood now.*

"Thank you, madam, we manage. Only if she needs to go to the hospital I may telephone for you to arrange transport. You will not mind?"

"Of course I should be glad . . . Does she understand about Angela? Last time I did not know what to say."

"I do not think she understands, madam. Please do not talk about Angela if you can help it. She keeps on asking for letters, especially if she sees a blue aerogram. So sometimes I read her my daughter Lilian's letters, only leaving the children out. Of course Angela had no children. It is not easy changing the Kikuyu words. I do not like to deceive her, but she will not rest otherwise."

"It all seems so sad: we cannot force the knowledge on her. And Angela's husband was also killed, you said?"

"Yes, in the same accident. There was a cable. I have to open her letters because now she cannot read handwriting, only big print like the books you bring from the library, and I dared not read it to her. I asked Councillor Mwangi for advice and he said the doctor had better be here in case she collapsed when she heard the news. So we asked the doctor to come, and he tried to explain to her about the accident, but she kept saying, 'So they will be here soon: isn't that good news?' He gave her sleeping pills, but she has stayed just the same. Even when Nigel telephoned from Australia, she kept saying Angela was coming and he had to speak to me because he could not understand her, although he has been here, you remember, since she had the stroke."

"But do not other people write?"

"Not many. I have to change her sisters' letters a bit when I read them."

"Perhaps it is a mercy," said Mrs. Banerjee, and pretended to arrange the cups and spoons and little plates with embroidered napkins.

Mrs. Smith looked up and saw Mrs. Banerjee's fine sculptured head interrupting her reverie.

"Have you heard from Nigel, Mrs. Smith?"

Oh yes, she had heard. Some weeks ago. Martha would remember. They were very well, oh yes, Nigel and Ann. Ann had gone back to teaching now that the boys were old enough – yes, big and fair like their grandfather, outdoor men, she supposed, though Adelaide was a big town, of course. Mrs. Smith didn't think she would go there now. She had put it off and off, and now travelling was a bother. Besides, Angela would be coming.

"Indeed?"

Oh yes, she had written to say so, her husband too. Doctors do not get much holiday but you have to look for a locum. Of course they had no children, so that made travelling easier.

"Certainly," agreed Mrs. Banerjee, although she was happy herself to have no less than eight grandchildren. But she had not seen the three in Canada. "The expense, these days, you understand . . ." She remembered enthusiastically her first sight of Nigel, when Mrs Smith had brought him to school in his little Moses basket. But she had been very conscious of Nigel even from the first signs, having just weaned her third, who was to be, as it turned out, her last. Of course, she had married very young, immediately after graduation. She giggled – glancing across at the poinsettia, the exact, vibrant red of her wedding sari, recapturing the breathless weight of the jewellery upon her nose, ears, forehead, the droning chant to keep down questions as

46

they circled the fire, cloth-linked, the surprise as the drape-
ries were lifted to give the first glimpse of her husband.

*"Mr. Banerjee was always good to me," she remarked
defensively. "He did not mind me taking some classes once I
was sufficiently recovered from childbirth. He used to take
us out to the Lake on Sundays and not mind if the children
made a noise. He would have been very happy to see
Uhuru . . ."*

*Both ladies pondered their teaching days separately, un-
til the ritual of tea was over and Mrs. Banerjee was able to
retreat. The memories were the happiest part of the afternoon.*

Ellen used generally to take the car. On days when
Jack needed it, for a meeting in town or buying stores, he
would run her down to the junction to get a lift from Mr.
Galsworthy, who went into Nakuru every day to look after
his insurance business. He and his wife and children lived
with Mr. and Mrs. Holmes, his sister and brother-in-law,
who ran a dairy. The bigger children used the guest *banda*
and they all messed together for economy. Mr. Galsworthy
professed himself delighted to be of assistance, but Ellen
did not feel comfortable about asking favours, compounded,
often enough, by offers of lifts from schoolboys' fathers once
she got to town. She would have to go after school to sit in
the bleak waiting-room, like a dentist's, perhaps getting
some marking done while Mr. Galsworthy settled with his
clients.

Ellen felt more at home in the classroom than on the
farm. Railings, corridors, registers, ladies' staff-room,
where the three of them were strictly segregated from the
male teachers unless there was a meeting, were all familiar. Mrs. Mistri, the Parsee, beautifully groomed, speaking
elegant English, could have been any of her former

colleagues transfigured by marriage. (Why had she not been transfigured herself?) Miss Ismail, whose father also taught in the school, waiting to go to India for her degree course, was shy to the point of nonentity. Mrs. Banerjee came in occasionally, to make a fourth, offering Indian music as an extra. Times were hard: the parents would have been more likely to pay up for book-keeping or even French.

This would have been the time to get to know Mrs. Banerjee and Mrs. Mistri better. In later years the mixed staff room, the more complex duties, the growing families, inhibited them. But there was so much delicate ground to traverse first – what one was accustomed to eat, to wear, to discuss outside the family, the obligations to kin, the religious analogies that prompted behaviour – that they hardly reached the point of personal intimacy. Mr. Banerjee seemed so old and set in his ways, Ellen wondered what, if anything, the two of them could find to talk about. He did not encourage visits to his wife's parents in Mombasa. Mrs. Mistri had a set speech about the beauties of Bombay. How could you know what heartbreak she had left behind?

Ellen grew fond of her little boys – some not so little: too old, in her view, for the material offered, able to take in something tougher. They sorted themselves out into individuals before her eyes – by voice, manner, face, talent – long before they grouped themselves into families or communities.

She wrote to Mr. L. S. B. Leakey, as the newspaper invited, about his course of lectures on Native Law and Custom, but was not able to go down to Nairobi because of school. She had marking and preparation to do – thank God she had brought her books. Not all of them were useful here but better, at least, than Wren and Martin's red abomination of a grammar and the model essays and sit-work that

48

the boys delighted in. So it was often easy to refuse to accompany Jack for a natter (which meant a good few bottles) at one of the neighbouring farms. They mulled over the site of the new Town Hall and extensions to the War Memorial Hospital. There was a minimum wage order for African staff, but it carried no sanctions and therefore had little impact. The Secretariat in Nairobi had burned down – to ashes, the newspaper had it – and people wondered what secret agreements and land transfers might have been consumed.

The image always stuck in her mind. The servants, one after another, had cooked on their little braziers in the quarters, and great flakes of ash or fragments of singed paper would float over into the backyard. Only Martha, who kept a respectful distance from the kitchen range even before she moved into the house to sleep, used it to warm her tea or vegetables. It was not only an economy but, Ellen thought, a ritual avoidance of that rapid heating of the charcoal and its gradual disintegration. Like the bloodheat which surged and consumed when you were young and then, as it cooled, fragmented the very substance of the fire, so that what heat remained was too fragile to put to use.

Bonfire night had always scared her – all right the pretty Catherine wheels but not the guy reeking and disintegrating in the flames. Perhaps she had a foresight of London burning, as the round chimed in discordant childish voices – but we have no water, but we have no water. Or perhaps because she had lived at low intensity her personal life had been consumed, like those long-dead leases and title-deeds, and only powdery ash remained of all that once had evoked desire, extravagance and appeals to law.

Jack was drinking too much, his interminable complaints about farm business not reasoned out into a form she could understand. In England he had been at a loss, needing her guidance. Here he had no such need and his hold on her slipped away. He thought her self-sufficient, as though her questions were for information, not a cry for help.

European news in the papers was frightening: they could not really assess it. Mummy's letters were only about the family, Father generally adding a postscript about the kind of work he was handling or local changes in Croydon. They did not actually bring home to you the feel of digging a hole for the air raid shelter in the garden or buying material for blackout curtains. They seemed not to anticipate the absurdity of barrage balloons hovering over the suburbs or snatching up your gas mask in a carrying case every time you ran over to the shops. Had England changed so much in a single year?

The advertisements in the *East African Standard* made you think of home. "It's fatal for a wife to look tired. Horlick's . . ." (That's not true, either. Who will notice how you look? No one. And though some might notice another girl who looked better, Jack was not one of that sort, in any case, who looked better? The one with the jaunty beret in the Du Maurier advertisement was not quite Rift Valley style either. And even in Happy Valley, she supposed, they didn't pull off their multiple aristocratic marriages by good looks but by the sheer weight of sexual experience.) Did *they*, perhaps, smoke De Reszke? She could not think of anyone else in East Africa who was likely to. In those days you could get Players in Kenya – Players please, the healthy sailor beaming from the poster. Now you only see local blends with a health warning on the packet. She had given all her albums of cigarette cards to Stanley when he was a little boy. Who had them now, she wondered. Probably nobody cared for cigarette cards any more. (In fact they were collectors' items.)

Old men – or not so old – in the Stag's Head would bring out their stories of "last time", the Tanganyika campaign and the defence of the railway, but now there were no Germans left . . .

Martha had not done the washing up yet. Sometimes her knees would not obey her as they used to. She would keep going of course. There was no alternative, but she prayed that the weakness would not come upon her when Mrs. Smith was in particular need.

Of course it would not. God was good: he added to your strength when you were responsible for others, like when the baby was tearing you apart. "It will stretch a mile before it splits an inch." *Her eyes strayed over the ground picking out every point of colour rather than let her mind wander to ask all over again, "What will happen to me if I have a stroke like her?"*

In the dust, a twist of potato peel. How did it get there? The chickens must have broken loose – yes, there was a day she had failed to shut the side gate properly and had to call a girl from the farm settlement to help her catch them. Father would never have allowed that. In his kitchens the rubbish-bin was always tightly closed, the barrier between employer's garden and the household offices absolute. Of course, that was not so at home, where growing things was more important than anything else. The peel took on the colour of school khaki; how she had laboured to fit the children out after Njogu had gone! So long as he lived he had always listened to reasonable requests. Now she did not even know whether Stephen, her first son, who had gone to

Mombasa and got lost, had yet caused Njogu to be born again. And did Stephen still bear that terrible heat?

Perhaps, after all, hot weather could be a blessing. The cold water stung her hands so sharply these days that she wondered how she would manage if they got all bent up like Mrs. Smith's. She kept a kettle hot to take the chill off as often as she could. It reminded her of the circumcision day. Her father was furious when he found out, but her mother said she must be prepared for marriage like other girls, and of course father was away a lot of the time.

She could not really remember the pain now, only it seemed absurd that when life had so much necessary pain in it you should inflict some extra just for the hell of it. When William, her youngest child, was born, the midwife told her she was luckier than those young mothers who had come after her and been savagely cut on a tide of reaction. She pitied them indeed if the pangs were worse than her own.

Martha herself, suddenly the focus of attention, had seen no reason to protest when her mother had insisted on the circumcision, perhaps thinking she was upholding some female power in the land by doing so. The event had bound her to some of the other girls and some of the old ladies, but it was no longer big enough to bind her to village and community. Her mother was behind the times. What could have bound her was the freedom oath.

But the oath was not offered to young girls, and her mother (it seemed from later hints and half statements) did not think it was properly administered. Only after seven years of marriage did Martha drink the first oath, and refuse to involve herself further, saying she must have her husband's permission, must not endanger his freedom of movement in his work, for in those days it was the most precious freedom of all.

"You have known Mrs. Banerjee a long time?" she ventured to ask, as Mrs. Smith opened her eyes.

"Oh yes, a long, long time. Since 1939. You were a little girl then, Martha?"

"I was a big girl but not yet married, helping my mother at home." Mrs. Smith closed her eyes again and luxuriated in memory.

She taught for nearly a year, became used to it, did not really want to get away, except a few days for shopping in Nairobi in August, that August when the world hung in the balance. She did not even consider Jack's suggestion that they could get a week or two in Mombasa while things were quiet and Uncle could cope. Everyone around insisted that you had to get down to sea-level. But Uncle said he hadn't been off the plateau for fifteen years and was none the worse for it.

"It doesn't do to make comparisons," he said, looking straight at her. "Only upsets people. In for a penny, in for a pound, that's the best way."

Her eyes were all for letters and newspapers, yet when the news of war actually broke in September it seemed un-real and far away. There were committees – for Red Cross, War Work, National Savings – but even in England nothing much seemed to be happening. Here also they had ration books and blackout curtains, though it was hard to see why.

The top primary classes seemed to grow before her eyes. The teachers pondered which ones would be able to go away to secondary school – Nairobi, Kisumu or Mombasa. Not all of those who passed well, of course. That was the same as in England. But they must find a way for Narendra. Surjit's family would certainly back him. Din deserved a place if only he didn't make any of his silly mistakes out of nervousness. Lakhani would go to India in any case.

Suddenly the morning tea went sour on her. After a moment's hesitation she bolted for the toilet. "Are you all right, dear?" Mrs. Banerjee was hovering, smiling. Suddenly she *knew*. Realised she had known for nearly a month. Surged with happiness.

She gave in her notice as soon as the doctor confirmed the pregnancy. Jack laughed at her excitement, but he was a bit excited himself and stopped poring openly over advertisements of cars for sale. She told Uncle she would be leaving work at the end of the term and he nodded sagely.

It would be a boy. She knew. Wrote to only a few, but everyone seemed to know, even Stanley, dead bored in France, waiting for a chance to hang out the washing on the Siegfried Line. Dead bored. She had not taken the newspaper notices very seriously. It made no sense for Kenya to be at war. The memsahibs and the honourables were always looking for something to start a committee about. You only had to say boo and the Italians would turn and run. The wireless said so.

Slowly it dawned on her that Jack looked to other people like a young man. He was going to be sent to fight the Italians. All round her farmers were looking for bailiffs and supervisors. They were lucky to have Uncle. Jack might not be home when the baby was born, though of course he said it would all be over in three months. "Over by Christmas," Stanley had said, but Christmas was practically here, and how was a nineteen-year-old dental student going to know anyway?

The months dragged by. Jack had to kit up and go — only to a training camp at first. Kimalel's son, Felix, went too: it was an adventure for strong, young men and opportunity to send pay home, learn a trade, try yourself out. They were not being forced like last time, though some people said they were being more than encouraged.

She did think about Jack – yes, of course she did – though the baby was a more constant and demanding presence. It was not so much the actual fighting but the thirst of the bare desert lands, the dry dust rubbing everything, his poor, fair, reddened skin, the coarse wool, his underlying shyness exposed to the public life of mess and patrol, his awkwardness with African employees that made her wonder how he would get along in that rough, masculine setting, so far from refills of petrol or water for the engines. Some of the officers would be trying to show they were a cut above, some of the men too (she sensed, though it was not yet permissible to say so) trying themselves out in a situation remote from the restraints of tribe or family.

The strange thing was that these black men, most of whom in Kenya could hardly feel their homes threatened in the way they might have been last time by Tanganyika, should be creeping over dry river-beds, in accordance with orders, or in the shadow of thorny bushes. Their opponents might have the fervour of defending their homeland – or they might not, if they realised how much fairer the English would be to them than the Italians. That they would be fairer she could not allow herself to doubt, but how would you *know* that, labouring on a plantation or unloading cargo in a port? The devil you knew might seem preferable.

She thought about Jack, but she did not fret over him as her mother fretted over Stanley. After all, her mother had memories of last time which had become remote to the daughters, only sentimental songs, intrusive poppies, fatherless schoolmates: memories of Tommies and Germans taking pot shots at one another in France instead of heading for a definite objective, men drowning in mud, crucified on the wire. Well, East Africa would never be like that. It all seemed far away, until she was in her eighth month and Stanley was spread-eagled on the beach at Dunkirk, his life bleeding away without hope of cover while those ahead of him queued patiently knee-high in water – "Next twenty forward. Here you are, sir. Any more for the Skylark?"

She did not think of it any more than she could help, must not expose Nigel to risk, perhaps could give him Stanley as a second name (for they had agreed that the baby would be Nigel or Angela) but Jack had not got the news yet. And he must not be made fearful on her account or encouraged to brood upon the nature of risk.

Some of the schoolboys and their parents came up to her in town with strange, formal condolences about Stanley, and she loved them for it. Mr. R. J. Patel sent a letter in the name of the board. Njoroge, prompted by Kirui, to whom she had explained her tears, gave a little speech full of Swahili bible texts on behalf of the staff.

Meanwhile there was the labour force to see to, bright letters to write home, not to make their burden even heavier, and Uncle flagging, so that you had to remind him more often to pay the men, order the feed supplements, and scrounge the petrol. All the same he laboured, in his ancient, spidery hand, to write a letter of sympathy to her parents for Stanley, praising her and promising to look after her.

She went to stay with a teacher at the European School a few days before the baby was due, and bore him in the War Memorial Hospital, surprised to have pulled it off without any kin around her. They used to regard Mother as

ineffectual, but somehow she had gone through this battle
of creation four times, brought them all through to
adulthood, fiercely maintained her simpering standards at
whatever cost – it now occurred to Ellen for the first time –
of home dressmaking and renovation. Someone else might
have let the music lessons go or held them back from Girl
Guide camps, but she would have scorned that as defeat.
What would she not give to have Mother beside her now?

Uncle came to drive her slowly and carefully home. He
was entranced by the baby but scared to touch him. Kirui
beamed and fussed and wanted to bring an ayah. She needed no ayah, did not want to let Nigel for a minute out of her
hands, but allowed Njoki to wash the nappies and scrub
around the cot in case Kirui should feel offended.

Surely, here they were safe from the stridency of war.
Until that loud-mouthed Irish woman, teaching at Turi,
was bound over for defeatism, breathing racial hatred
against not the blacks but the Jews, as though that made
any difference.

Jack managed to get a few days at home. It was good to
have him there for a bit, clumsily enraptured with Nigel,
reviving some of the old vigour in Uncle, calling the staff to
fresh attention, familiar and wordless in bed. She suspected
a kindly censorship in his account of the campaign: the dust
and flies were a nuisance, some of the African NCOs really
very smart, could challenge some of our own to pull their
socks up, air bombardment a bit nerve-racking at times:
you could see the old crates swinging about in the air
currents but that gave you plenty of time to duck. He said
nothing to betray the stress of man-to-man combat, no
"don't shoot till you see the whites of their eyes".

"You probably heard Parker got it?"

Yes, she had seen the obituary in the paper and the war swooped suddenly close. He was a crony of Jack's who had sometimes stopped by to visit them. "Got too close to a land-mine. Lost his driver as well and one of the best Luo corporals. Playing silly buggers – whether it was the driver or the chap who marked the edge is hard to tell."

"Don't do anything like that, will you, Jack?"

"Not on your life. I want to tell the tale to young Nigel one of these days."

They could never be more explicit than that but for the time being, it was something to hold on to.

Chapter 4

As Uncle grew weaker, Ellen found she had to trust Njoki more with the baby. He did not change his routine but would leave breakfast half-eaten and wander out to the farm, get the men started on a job and forget to tell them when to stop (cutting fencing, perhaps, or dipping sheep).

Njoroge would more and more often use his own judgment and come to tell Ellen what they had decided. Uncle would not have a doctor, complained of no pain. He kept a hurricane lamp burning all night so that he could read if he felt restless. He would point out the same newspaper article that had struck his fancy three or four times. Some afternoons he would sit dozing in his chair with the wireless turned on, although the programmes, Home and Empire, came in the mornings and evenings.

Kirui would have to persuade him to change his knitted cardigan, where the food had spilt, or his sweaty socks. At other times he would hand over, shamefaced, a bundle of linen to be washed. He still signed the cheques and insisted on checking the deposit book before he did so, but he sometimes forgot that Kirui and ayah were his responsibility too while Jack was away, and these days the farm workers had to come to the verandah for their pay.

One day in October, Ellen had taken Nigel into Nakuru to show him off in the staff room. She had a Moses basket secured to the back seat of the car and now felt quite confident about handling the baby. The teachers complained of being snowed under. Extra children had come from Mombasa where the schools were still closed on a war alert, and some from Nairobi, though only the boarding schools had been evacuated from the capital. Nigel was gurgling happily to himself when they got home and opened the house. Uncle had slipped sideways in his chair, his mouth sagging open and a hoarse noise coming from his throat. Ellen shouted for help as she placed Nigel in his cot, then drove in haste to the Holmeses to ring the doctor. By the time she got back it was all over, and she marvelled that she had not panicked. The doctor helped to lay out the body and explained what she had to do about the funeral. Coolly, next day, she went to see the chaplain, ordered the coffin, put a notice in the paper, and sent a wire to Jack. Everything was under control.

Half a dozen of the farm workers made their way to the cemetery – they were not allowed into the church, of course – and stood around silently. The older of the neighbouring farmers attended: the younger were away at the war. One of the wives offered to come and stay with Ellen for a few days but she shook her head. Uncle had been so skeletally present for so long that she did not feel a big change, though in days to come she would miss the old man's silent presence, his weight of experience, the sense of family. A lawyer introduced himself and made an appointment to come and see her. It was no good asking whether Jack could have got away. She did not know where he was or how long a message would take to reach him.

She had the old man's chair moved into the abandoned bedroom. She gave his old clothes to Kirui to share with the men. There wasn't much else – a watch and chain, a family bible, an old chessboard and a set of *The Modern Home Handyman*, a German tin helmet from the First World War, a couple of campaign medals, some photographs and old letters in an inlaid box, a cup from some distant gymkhana and a battered first aid kit. She did not give a thought to the furniture or the china. This was not like

England where everything precisely belonged to somebody. She had no very clear idea what the lawyer was coming for.

Nigel was screaming when the strange car trundled up to the gate. She pulled off her waterproof apron and pushed her hair into place while Njoki took him somewhere out of earshot and Kirui served tea with scones she had made last week and sealed in a tin. (She was still varying the recipe with altitude the Church of Scotland book told you. Without a man to feed, perhaps she need not bother next time.)

"Ah, Mrs. Smith," said Mr. Herring with some embarrassment. "Sorry about your sad loss especially when – ah – Jack is away at the war, but he had a word with me, you know, when he was here last, and saw the way things were going. He said you would take care of everything. Put it in writing in case he – ah – was posted overseas or anything."

She smiled deprecatingly. What did she not take care of? Nigel's wails were still audible. He was the one most in need of her care. "The late Mr. Smith has deposited a will with me. Perhaps you did not know that?"

"No, I didn't know; he shared everything with my husband – I never thought . . ."

The dresser, the old blue and white china, the serviceable furniture: it had just come . . . She had never asked . . . Panic must have been showing in her eyes.

"Do not be alarmed, Mrs. Smith. The position is not too bad. I would not say rosy, but not too bad. The will divides the property between your husband and his mother, except for a couple of personal items (an old army comrade, a lady in Nairobi, fifty pounds each.) But I understand that your mother-in-law no longer has her own household. Even if she had wanted anything of – ah – sentimental value from the

61

house, the times are not propitious for sending . . . There will be just a little cash at bank, not more than a hundred or so after these bequests, so Jack's half will see you clear of the funeral and the documents, not much more.

"Now a half share of the farm is Jack's already. I will prepare an account of what remains to be divided. That means you couldn't sell it without Mrs. Smith's consent – even if you got that, it is not a good time to sell. If you did, and cleared yourself of the mortgage, you would have to include all the furniture and effects, at this time rather hard to replace . . . So you will have to hold on, I should say, and put a quarter of income into her account."

He bumbled on and Ellen had an overwhelming sense of relief. Daddy was looking after Mrs. Smith's affairs. Could you actually remit funds to Britain in the middle of a war? Even on half of what Mr. Smith used to give her, they would manage.

She wrote to Jack, wrote to Daddy, asked the solicitor for his bill. Jack had been in his gruff way fond of the old man. He wrote back bemoaning the loss of the only relation who had given him a chance and telling her to use her discretion. Everything had better be put in her name in case he should meet his death in action. This instruction Mr. Herring duly translated into a tidy will to be signed on his next leave.

Daddy, of course, replied meticulously:

"My dear Ellen,

We sympathise with you and Jack on the sad loss of your uncle. I am sorry you had to make all the arrangements yourself but that is all too often the lot of women in wartime.

We are, thank God, well here, except that your mother ricked her ankle when we had to rush to the shelter one night last week when a lot of flak was going up and down. London has been badly hit, as you must know from the news, but our nearest bomb was half a mile away, though one of the air raid wardens died in Downs' Road after being hit by a big lump of shrapnel. Mavis is able to come and help Mother in the house while she keeps her foot up.

Now I have written to your mother-in-law about your uncle's will, but have not been able to go and see her because of Mother's accident. In any case, it seems likely that the home will have to be evacuated because of heavy bombing on the south and east coast. I am sure Jack must have written to his mother to break the news of her brother-in-law's death.

The will I drew up for her shares her estate between Jack and his sister, with a small bequest to Mrs. Ashton who was so providentially instrumental in bringing you and Jack together. Of course, the proceeds of the house were used for an annuity, but she still has some cash at bank and I should advise her to leave this and the jewellery to her daughter and sister and the East African property to Jack, since it is hard to forecast whether the channels of transmission will stay open. (We have removed signposts so that parachutists will be confused in the event of invasion. The intention is sound, but I doubt if we should have much fear of an enemy force that could not on practice distinguish between Birmingham and Stratford-on-Avon. However we do not intend to let Fritz – as we used to call him – get so far.)

Believe me, we consider ourselves fortunate to have two of our girls and their children away from the main theatre of war. Give our love to little Nigel and assure Jack that we expect the allied campaign in East Africa to be short and sweet, in contrast to last time, so that he may soon be home to look after you.

Your ever loving,

Father.

Ellen sniffed back a few tears over the letter. Air raid panic in *Surrey*? Evacuation from sunny *Worthing*? Her college friends all congratulated her on being safe. What did they know about danger? Snakes – one of her neighbours had miscarried after an encounter with a spitting cobra – forest fires – malaria – blackwater fever.

Musa's accounts were not very enlightening:

By sale of milk . . .

By sale of livestock . . .

To purchase of animal feed . . .

To Standard Bank of South Africa . . .

This last item was the mortgage, nearly one third of income if you averaged it out over wet and dry months. Jack had made a standing order to be paid to her monthly in lieu of Uncle's housekeeping money. She tried not to touch her savings.

In fact, events forestalled the calculations. The Old Ladies' Home was never evacuated. A direct hit removed it and most of the occupants. Condolences were exchanged and Jack's sister was only too glad to accept Mr. Mountford's suggestion about her mother's will. They would have been better off if it had not been for increased wartime taxes and an honorarium to Mr. Holmes for keeping an eye on the staff.

The rough untended corner of the garden reminded Ellen of the struggle to keep things tidy during those years Jack was away, the devastation in wartime London which she would later see, (though then already ordered, planned for, taken for granted), the desultory sequence of her own life. Here were white pebbles that someone, Nigel perhaps, had fixed into a fancy border which long ago over-stretched its boundaries. A straggle of fern – a bird's water-dish

knocked askew – a torn bootlace. It took a special grace to be
"a clean worker", one in whose kitchen the washcloths were
always hung out to dry, the left-overs disposed of, the
sleeves never bedraggled. In real life there was always
some effect spilling over.

After Uncle died, Ellen had to pay out wages and help
Musa with bills for stores and the endless form-filling that
went with wartime control of crops. She wrote to Jack about
the big decisions. There was no more blackout after the
liberation of Somaliland: it seemed absurd to expect attack
from the air on these millions of empty acres. What was the
point of risking men's lives to destroy fields full of stubborn
crops? (In Bengal and the Ukraine the allies could have told
her, without even asking the enemy.)

Jack got some leave in 1942. "A little dust-up," he said,
dragging a foot in plaster, "sort of thing that could happen
in peace-time, really." He meant to comfort her. In fact she
was hardly more alarmed for his hurt than relieved that he
should be, for a time withdrawn from the wear and tear.
They managed to get a few days in Nairobi, going by train,
he proud of his injury, she of her baby. The place still looked sophisticated compared with Nakuru, though imported
goods were in short supply and the streets full of uniformed
Europeans. A. T. S., people said with a wink, meaning the
big hotels, Avenue, Stanley, Torrs, where the officers booked in with their female aides and drivers from the Auxiliary
Territorial Service. Well, there were not likely to be any
glamorous service women in the rough spots where Jack
stood guard. He had to make up for lost time and Ellen was
delighted to find herself again pregnant. Angela preened
herself and sidled in the womb, without the same weight of
astonishment as a first baby.

And Nigel, running confidently, speaking each day more formal and imaginative words, filling the rest of her horizon and the weekly letters home, helped her round out and blossom with a new certainty. Mrs. Galsworthy, after enough practice runs to give confidence, took Nigel in for the week his mother went to have the baby. He did not take it too badly, though of course he clung close. The farm people were charmed with Angela. Kirui excelled himself with milk puddings and purees.

On the farm, rationing had not hit them much. But 1943 was a year of drought. As Angela grew fat and learned to smile, the maize dried and stopped at shoulder height. Tiny cobs, sheathed in brown papery leaves drooped on brittle upright stalks. Grass withered: you used precious water to coax the kale to grow for the cows, let women take the unripe cobs for grinding while men opened the field for cattle to browse on the maize refuse. You were supposed to burn the stalks immediately after harvest to keep off attacks of the maize stalk borer, but this year there was no harvest to mark the season. Jack and Uncle had thought of buying one of the advertised "mould board ploughs pulled easily by 12 oxen on old land when not very wet". They had decided against it because the hire of the oxen might cost as much as easing the ancient tractor along for another season. But old, long broken ground, not very wet – there was plenty of that about. You bought in cattle feed from the sugar cane zones and the swamps and staved off the bank. The dry earth of the potato ridges crumbled. The wisest of the staff planted melons and gourds and onions to tunnel down for moisture deep below the ground.

Government reduced the standard ration of maize meal to farm workers from two pounds to one and a half daily, and their wives were not called on for seasonal work because there was nothing for them to harvest, and next to nothing to weed. Now handling the money herself, Ellen came to see how little their wages were, observing in the town shops her pupils sprang from how long it would take a labourer to save up for a lamp, a blanket, or a hoe. To cut rations as well was more than she could bear. She had taught, after all, sons of grocers and wholesale merchants, and was expected to go back and teach them again. She combed the town for extra flour, bargained over black market prices, offered advice on textbooks and handwriting. She managed to keep up the two pounds a day and Njoroge discreetly let her know that the men, for all that they were still suffering, were grateful. Some farmers tried to do the same, but it was too much for those with thousands of acres and manpower to match. Others said they had enough losses already: workers must take the rough with the smooth and see if they could work miracles with their own squatters' acre, for goodness sake. It was not quite as bad as the thirties, the Galsworthys said, because people had the war bonus subsidies of the last couple of years to fall back on, and there were wartime jobs for the younger farmers and their wives if they really failed. "Then it was the Italian invasion of Ethiopia that kept us going," Joe Holmes grinned, "boom time in Nairobi; supplying their army. Now another boom time getting their army out. Maybe they'll have to come back to bail us out again after this lot's over."

Ellen felt sick. She had never thought of that before. Mr. Holmes had applied for an Italian prisoner mason to help rebuild his dairy and store - cheap skilled labour. The "collaborators" were kept under tight discipline and were glad to have something to do. But right now, the cows needed fodder more than they needed improved quarters.

The next year, the government urged another fifteen per cent cut in labour rations where it could be done without detriment to the war effort. (The "war effort" for farmers was defined as "producing larger quantities of scheduled crops at controlled prices".) In 1940 the conscription officer had said that this could only be done by giving better rations to both conscripted and voluntary labour, and the farmers had agreed. Now she saw that this was one of those flagship statements meant to flutter in the breeze and then be forgotten. Like "Singapore shall not fall".

"If the war effort means keeping the bloody country going you don't improve it by starving people," pronounced Jack when he came, and she felt a surge of love for him. (Where did the love, then, come from? Could it not be taken for granted as Mother and the prayer-book said?) He was not going to encourage any damned ignorant trade unions. He had a right to the land he had inherited from his uncle: he had not bargained for it with honey or blankets or begged any bastard in the civil service to give it to him. He had paid his taxes and mortgage like a man. But the least any feller could expect was a full belly after a full day's work.

God knows how many mouths it had to feed, but the workers got their two pounds a day.

Martha too spent some time gazing at the ground and picking out patterns, keeping a distant eye on Mrs. Smith in her wheel-chair. It went against the grain just to sit: one ought to be knitting or weaving baskets. But the grandchildren were already over-supplied with woollies and there was no longer the give and take of neighbourhood. She grew tired too, frighteningly tired, at the end of all the cleaning and cooking and persuading – "Shall I get in another packet of tea-leaves?" – "Will you not change your petticoat?" –

"Let us check through the linen cupboard in case Angela comes."

Her wages were always paid promptly into the bank, and she got enough money for housekeeping: the lawyer would see to that as long as she presented a tidy expenditure list. One of the retired ladies would sit in for her once a month when she went to the bank, and they got on all right provided madam did not go in for extravagances – a violet dressing-gown, shiny and hard to wash, she had insisted on buying once when Mrs. Mistri took her into town – or they had to pay for extras like getting the fridge repaired or bringing a man to deal with termites on the verandah.

There was enough, she supposed, but nursed her own savings carefully for an end that must one day come and leave her homeless. She had finished paying off the little house in Nakuru, but there was no one she could trust to look after the plot of land for her, so that produced only a trifling sum compared with what you could get by really working at it. And these days you could buy off some of your responsibilities with money. She had once felt compelled to ask the lawyer – the grey-haired European one with the steel spectacles and a hurried manner – what would happen if Mrs. Smith had to go to hospital, and he told her that he could get in touch with Nigel in Australia if need be. Meanwhile, he said, they could get by without asking for help as long as she was careful. And careful she was, of course, by nature and had always had to be.

Those famine days, she remembered, during the war when Stephen was a little boy and Lilian had not yet been born. Two babies had miscarried between them. It was not that she was badly off, compared with others, with Njogu bringing something at the end of the month and sometimes managing a quick visit when the lorry paused for a day or two in Nairobi between those endless trips ferrying goods from the coast. There were not many buses in those days and no time to walk. It was a matter of knowing people on the road.

He had slapped her once – generally his hand was not heavy – when he saw how Stephen's legs had dwindled and his belly protruded. Maybe he had eaten dirt with the other children even if he was less desperately hungry than they. Surely Njogu must know that you could not keep it all for yourself, the food he brought, even if you stored some away to give to the child in the night or bolt down yourself at cock-crow, fearful that without that little hoarded cold *uji*, the last hunk of that bread brought a week ago from the town, you would not face the long dry day, clearing the field, grubbing up any fallen grains, willing the burden to lodge itself more firmly in your womb. Sunken eyes watched everything that came in and pestered you for a share of what remained. But she had managed. Later, in her widowhood, she had still managed, and even today, now that she was alone.

Stephen was lost, Lilian far away, William governed by that wife of his . . . Her sisters-in-law had gone their own way, out of sight. Her father's remaining relatives, her younger brother and two sisters, were remotely in touch, but more often needing help than ready to give it. She could no longer take time off to meet them at Nakuru Bus Park if they were passing through, and they had never found their way out to the house, though Mrs. Smith, these days, would not have minded. Occasionally they sent news of a funeral, a wedding, a harambee. She also was not familiar with all their houses.

Ellen watched Martha out of half-closed eyes. She must be getting old too, and it was harder for her than for a Euro-

70

pean to be far from her children. Martha had had a hard life. Ellen realised that she had been fortunate in those who served her. Kirui had welcomed her gradually into the kitchen he had made his own, and kept his temper through those hard times of drought.

Kirui went on leave and came back thin and subdued: he asked for an advance on wages and spent a long time in Nakuru negotiating with someone who could carry food to the home place. From Ukambani, men flocked westward looking for work (since movement to the coast was restricted) and whole families migrated. At the same time, Mediterranean shores were liberated from the Axis and newshounds anticipated the second front. Two ounces of butter a week per person in Britain and tinned goods, if there were any, on points. But in Britain you did not see the fields devastated round you any more than you saw the oily surge under which a merchant ship had sunk to the bottom: convoys were not allowed to stop and hunt for survivors. Could it be true that anyone went hungry in the fine air of Greece or in concentration camps close to the cultural heartland of Europe?

Angela grew bonny, slurped cereals with milk and honey, whooped joyfully over mashed avocado pear and pawpaw. Nigel was grown-up, spooning his own breakfast egg, expending his small pocket money when they went into town. Njoki had gone away to get married, so Kirui brought his daughter Mary, a half-starved girl who did not look strong enough to scrub nappies. But some mystery occurred, which Kirui preferred not to discuss, and Mary was spirited away again. Then there was Lucy, who had been chased away by her husband for not having children, and she suited more or less, and had nowhere else to go.

A week or two after Jack came home, demobbed with some of the other group IIs whose older men folk were no longer able to work in the farm, the Education Officer renewed his attack, and Mrs. Smith consented to go back to school. He had been tactful, considering that the papers were full of acrimonious letters about the shortage of teachers and nurses, but although some of them were signed, unashamedly, "Working Mother", the worst excesses of the Woman Power Ordinance could not force you away from your baby. But Ellen was glad to hand back to Jack the unbearable problems of the farm, and he needed time to get to know the children properly. Angela was eighteen months, staggering around making wild swipes at Nigel's toys: at three and a half he did not always take this graciously. Besides, they would have to get along without Jack's service pay, though for the moment there would be a couple of months' leave and a gratuity. But there was a more positive inducement even than the money. The school was now taking girls.

They came in all shapes and sizes of body, mind and background. It was like a new world peeping through a scalloped shell-edge waiting to be opened. They all managed to get along in English of a kind. Some were joining the higher classes, having learned the basics in Nairobi or Kisumu. Earnest square-jawed Sikhs (Kaur they were all called, to distinguish them from boys of the same personal names), business-like, intent on understanding and being understood, excellently nourished and disciplined, some of the older ones, she later found out, terrified that an engagement might have been entered into without their knowledge. Hindus, a lifelong expense to their families – no one handed out sweetmeats at *their* arrival – whose skins soon became pallid with fasting, cosmetics and late nights.

72

Prettiness and finery were of great importance to them (every excuse pleaded to avoid wearing uniform even for half a day) but they took second place to a good name. You could not send them on an errand where they would remain for an instant alone with a male teacher or student. At first there was constant fuss about taking them home. Then they took to walking in a big group, heedless of distraction but not unaware of being noticed. The Parsees and a few of Ismaili girls had English-speaking mothers and high-class English manners to match. The Muslims were shy and not too cohesive because of their various denominations.

Together, they led Mrs. Smith to strain her ears, listening more intently than the boys had demanded to the various cadences of English, the hidden meanings that lurked in the corners of words, look for in find, crave for in like, have been told to be careful of in hate. Most came from merchant or artisan homes and had been more closely kept than their brothers. These were the guinea-pigs, watched and scolded, often taken out of school åt the plea of some religious aunt or hopeful suitor. They might become an asset to the shop, speaking English with customers, bashing cash registers. A few set their sights on teaching or nursing, instinctively aware of the value of money, and the chance to escape total domination. The Goans were more at home in the colonial world, short-haired and sophisticated. The lawyers' and doctors' daughters did not see the prospect of high school as a privilege; if it never opened they might be sent to Nairobi or Kampala or even overseas. To the others it was a marvel. No one had anticipated that these wisps of humanity would become matrons bringing up families in London, holding their own in assembly lines, asserting their caste in hospital kitchens and suburban greengrocers.

Ellen was sometimes glad she lived out of town. It was exciting, in a way, when one was shopping, the piercing whisper, "Madam, I should like you to meet my mother," the *namaste*, the careful platitudes by translation, the nervous, liquid eyes, the gifts that followed. But one felt at a disadvantage, apologising for the need to present change to this girl child, challenge if one could not transform her. At the mechanics' she was always afraid that Jack would cause offence, though he had the measure of the man-to-man relationship and seldom did so. The boys had a bigger basis of respect on which to stand. But now she came to love the girls, treasured their best essays and their Christmas cards – Lakshmi, Meena, Harbinder, Asha, Leila, Jita.

The war sort of petered out, since many of the East African forces were already back home. Symbolically the high point was the return of 67 African prisoners of war, taken at Tobruk, under their Company Sergeant Major Robert Okari, in January of 1945. A Settlers' Band played them ashore in a haze of loyalty and brotherhood and half envied what they had seen of Europe, moving largely from camp to camp. After that the rubble of Europe and the inferno of Hiroshima seemed very far away. Because a lot of the KAR were still in Burma, they played down VE Day and kept the main celebrations till the fall of Japan. It was not like Croydon, where the end of rocket attacks loomed larger than the continuation of ration books. There was a jolly party at the Club where they sang sentimental songs – someone said that Ellen looked like Vera Lynn – and toasted a new world, but not much speculation about what the new world would look like.

They thought – if they thought at all – that it would brighten up the desolate streets of Tyneside and soften the

74

scorched earth of Russia. It seemed to have nothing to do
with the fact that Felix – and good luck to him – was doing
an ex-service course in motor mechanics and would not be
coming back to the farm, or that the bright, young fellow
who replaced him would leave to become a trade union
organiser.

Some newspaper correspondents were furious that demobbed soldiers were running home to the reserves,
ignoring the rehabilitation that was being provided to fit
them back into civilian life. Did they still have to be
regimented into private choice? Elegant English letters
signed with African names made you doubt it. Ellen
delighted in news of her primary pupils who had managed
to get to secondary school in India: it did not occur to her
that they would see new nations being born there and bring
the idea home with them.

Since petrol was still a problem, she sometimes took a
ride in with Mr. Galsworthy and gave him something towards the expenses. War and drought had undermined
some of the more high and mighty British attitudes to
money and sex equality, though in fact Mr. Galsworthy was
doing all right. To claim war bonus on recommended crops,
you had to have them insured.

Mr. Galsworthy had a Goan clerk, a neat, skinny man
with a perpetually worried look. He would always make
sure there was somewhere for Mrs. Smith to sit, and confided that he had a baby boy who might one day be coming to
her school. The status of Goans was at the time indeterminate, and some considered themselves Portuguese. In Nairobi they had a school of their own. The Catholic church
liked to claim their diaspora, though half the people in Goa
were Hindu.

There was a language problem. Some teachers were inclined to flout the English medium rule and drop into Hindi at moments of stress. Goans did not learn Hindi, and no one else was eager to learn Konkani, a fearsomely complicated language. The baby boy was followed by a couple of sisters and at the end of 1945 Mr. de Souza announced that he was moving to Nairobi. There was a better job and above all, there was the Dr. Ribeiro Goan School. His wife's sisters also lived there. No one could object. And so came Mwangi.

Mwangi was a stocky fellow of middle height who always wore a collar and tie. Sometimes a jacket, sometimes a knitted pullover, sometimes an affair of zips and pockets, but inevitably a collar and tie, shoes with socks, and pressed trousers. Mwangi, Mr. Galsworthy explained, was replacing Mr. de Souza. Times had changed. These fellows needed to be given a chance. Excellent war record. (Also, the thought occurred to Ellen, he will not expect as much as 100 shillings a month. Mr. Galsworthy needs to economise. His wife, stringy, high-pitched, is desperate to take the children to England for education. She has been on edge ever since her mother was bombed out in London and moved to furnished rooms in Pinner. But passages are still hard to get, and goodness knows how they will fit into school in over-crowded, war-scarred Britain, on tight rations, among children old-eyed and heavy with experiences they have not shared. She thinks she will get a job easily, but ex- servicemen are trooping back into civilian life. Well, Mwangi is an ex-serviceman too and, whatever the reasons, it is good to give him a chance.)

Mwangi was polite, attentive. Mrs. Smith, he had been told, often needed to sit for a while and get on with her marking. There had been one of the officers, he remarked

76

discreetly, "up in Somalia. A Lieutenant Smith. Perhaps. . ."

"Choose another name," growled Mr. Galsworthy. "Smith is about as common as Mwangi. Ten in every platoon."

"Lieutenant J. Smith," persisted Mwangi. "He said that his wife was a teacher. That is why he was sure he could teach us a thing or two."

He knew, of course, and later would improve the occasion.

"Here the Gazette refers to the Licensing Bill, madam, but on the form it is printed *Licence*, with a *c*. Would you explain . . ."

"The word *principal* we use of a headmaster, but also when referring to stocks and shares . . . The difference between *dominion* and *colony* . . ."

Mwangi had completed standard six before the war broke out and always had a good report. He might have gone to train as a teacher, but he had thought it his duty, he said, to join up, and in the army he had kept close to the education officer and been posted to Signals. He had kept his ear open for the details of English speech, had been in Mogadishu and then in Madagascar with the rank of corporal.

Jack did not take much interest in Ellen's reports of Mwangi – "about as common as Smith" – but one day he called at the insurance office to intercept her. He had brought the car in for service and been invited to a sundowner at a friend's place. The two men immediately recognised one another and fell to reminiscing: they were still at it when Ellen dragged herself in from school, tired and untidy, after an afternoon bristling with question tags. Her ears whistled with rising sibilants.

"We are late . . ."

" Isn't it?"

"No, aren't we?, Now try again. We are hungry . . ."

"Aren't it?"

"Isn't we?"

"Get the right two together now: It is a fine day . . ."

"Isn't it?"

"Very good! Now: These are good apples . . ."

"Isn't it?"

"Aren't they? Now pay attention! These are good apples, aren't . . ."

"They?"

"But Angela . . ."

"We needn't be too late. Kirui got a lift in with me, so I told him to tell Njoki to give Angela her supper and let Nigel have his toy tractor from the cupboard. It's months since we've been anywhere together."

"Yes, it is. I'm sorry dear." (When did we ever go to places together? If I didn't have to work . . .) "But I wish I'd known. I could have brought a spare dress." (But the pink ·one needs washing. The two piece I've worn every time I've gone to the club since Angela was born.)

"Actually I had thought of that too. Lieutenant Smith always at the ready." Mwangi, to Ellen's astonishment, permitted himself to giggle. "It's your birthday next week and I've sold a couple of calves today, so why don't we go and look for some glad rags, as they say in Hollywood?"

Ellen could hardly hide her surprise.

"Are you married, corporal?" Jack bellowed suddenly.

Mwangi, who had leapt to his feet to give Ellen his chair, now transformed his shape and gave a smart salute.

"Permission to take steps, sah."

"It's a bloody drastic step to take, corporal."

"But necessary to the welfare of the force, sah."

"Discipline is essential, corporal."

"Well and good, sah."

"Stand easy. Tell Mr. Galsworthy the memsahib's gone with me, will you? Good to see you, Mwangi."

"I would say the same, sah. Enjoy the party."

"Good fellow, that," said Jack as they reached the pavement and decided where to start their shopping. "We were in a couple of the tight spots together. He may not be too fond of officers, but if the choice is between an Eytie and me, it's the Eytie that will bite the dust, I'm telling you. Straight between the eyes. He's a bloody wonderful marksman."

The shops were in no hurry to close. Ellen chose a blue chiffon blouse and a black skirt which, in obedience to reports of London fashion, came three inches below the knee. Since it was designed for Nakuru fashion, it was too big everywhere else and had to be belted tightly at the waist. You could always ring the changes on separates. (At least, so the magazines said. The blouse would hardly go with her pre-war tweed suit or the striped cotton skirt).

"Lovely," remarked Jack, paying cash.

Conversation at the sundowner was not brilliant but it made a change. Hector Munro of Dundori was in the news, praised as a model employer.

"Bourneville and all that. Make your labour love you. He'll be in trouble one of these days, you mark my words."

"Maybe, but his yields are good and his people stay with him."

"Good job they do, if they're going to expect community welfare schemes when they come to me looking for a job. I've got enough to do to make ends meet as it is."

"They prefer to be left alone, that's my theory. It's nothing *personal*, Mrs. Smith. Don't look so down in the mouth. After all, I went down to Mombasa with the old trombone to welcome those POWs – bloody marvellous (pardon my French). Glad to shake that Company Sergeant-Major by the hand. Let them have their vocational training-schemes for ex-servicemen by all means. But business is business. On my farm I'm boss."

"And on parade at dawn," laughed Jack. "Lucky me to have Vera Lynn on duty with me."

He couldn't get home quick enough. One of the good days.

Mwangi, Ellen discovered, was already married. No, not in church – that was for teachers and mission employees: if you were in private business it wasn't necessary. The old way of doing things left you more room for manoeuvre, didn't she think so? Truly she had never thought about it.

"You ask your Bwana, then. He used to tell us never to leave ourselves without a line of retreat."

That was as near to being cheeky as he ever came. Next time he showed her a photograph of a bouncy, pop-eyed baby girl.

"Marion Njoki, Mrs. Smith. Remember the name. She'll be in your school one of these days."

He was right, too.

The farm was looking up. In fact by the end of the war oats were being over-produced and they had to reschedule again. Produce prices were keeping up, cargo ships were now available and parts of Europe were still desperately in need of food, helped by the Marshall Plan to get their economies going. (Parts of Asia were also reviving their agriculture, but not on the same terms.) Cereals and canned meat were going like a dream, so the highlands could be happy. But the smell of real coffee burst upon beleaguered Europe like a whiff of Paradise, after years of burnt acorns, so those planters on the other side of the mountain also rejoiced. Someone proposed that African Cooperative Societies might join the Kenya Farmers's Association on the same terms as white ones: the motion was defeated, but it was not beyond the bounds of possibility. You could give them a foot in the door without the embarrassment of having to scrutinise applications from every Tom, Dick and Harry who had two acres in the reserve. But you had to be careful. That fellow Beauttah, with his fancy name and beautiful written English, had got himself accepted and even turned up at a meeting. You couldn't do with another cock-up like that. As for wearing a label marked "African" at the Show, it got them in cheap, after all.

There were some fragments of fluted shell on a bare patch of earth somehow shaded from the sun and rain. Could they really have come from the sea-side? Or was it a trick of the light on spilt bonemeal or that stuff you fed to debilitated chickens? You used to be encouraged to bring home wild flowers and bits and pieces to prove your interest in natural history. Now it was considered a sin to interfere with the ecological balance. But humanity survived by making inroads on to nature. And these days people interfered even with your intimate self, photographing your baby in the womb, plugging in hormones to counteract the change of life. The human abortion rate increased while people agonised over birds' eggs. Your exposure to sunlight was timed and a tour company programmed your leisure time.

By the end of 1946 Jack felt finances were secure enough to propose a holiday after the school closed for Christmas. In Kenya, you soon found out, a holiday meant Mombasa. Brave spirits might go up to Malindi – more "authentic" – they said (in relation to what?) – but that meant a tiresome bus journey, unless you were taking the car, and it was not much of a break coaxing the old jalopy over the road to the coast the way it was then. But you could go to Mombasa by train, taking out the daylight hours in Nairobi, with sleepers and meals laid on: not cheap, perhaps, but cheaper than another night at a hotel and the allure of an unfamiliar bar.

The children had never seen the sea and Ellen had been eight years inland. It seemed a hundred years away that Father and Mother had planned family holidays every summer. There was a world of choice, even after the unstated limits of expenditure had curbed the more fanciful dreams – a cruise to the Western Isles or boating on the Broads. They were considered too young to go abroad: actually it was perhaps the parents who doubted their own capacity, for poorer families bargained for passages to Boulogne and practised their French in shabby pensions behind the beach. The Isle of Wight had been her favourite, with a feel of real adventure in the boat journey and a ghost of Victorian elegance. Classy Bognor Regis had bored her to tears as she settled behind a book, scathing of charabanc rides and teatime orchestras. Mavis had demanded riding lessons, which cost a lot, and Stanley had been small enough to play with a bucket and spade on the bland, discreet beach. The year they had gone to the Lake District was better, and there

82

had been Penzance, but all this was obscured now by the workaday image of England, beacon and fortress.

Perhaps at last she and Jack were beginning the domestic routine she had been brought up to expect, and that seeing of the world that had long been reserved for service personnel and refugees.

The holiday was not all Ellen had hoped for, keeping the children amused through those dark hours on the train and in the heat of the hotel room, the bucket and spade on the beach routine threatened by the pounding energy of the ocean. Jack was again like a stranger, away from the familiar round, always running into "a fellow I met in the regiment", with whom he would plunge into long reminiscence at one bar or another, while she sat with the children and perhaps the other fellow's bored and brassy wife over ice-cream, waving away the vendors of shells, fruit and wooden carvings. Perhaps the magic of the family holiday had always been to have the parent securely at one's beck and call. Once or twice she could remember, when Beatrice was thought old enough to keep an eye on them, mother craving their permission to go downstairs and dance – dance! At their age! The girls had nodded, scandalised. Stanley was a good baby and asleep.

The port was dingy from wartime use, the fort closed off for official purposes. African movement was restricted "for economy" and people said labour unrest was brewing. How did you know, on a visit how would you ever know, except that most of these upcountry men were obviously far from home, food was dear and houses, even for Europeans, hard to come by? There had been strikes in Uganda for better wages and a war bonus, but people said they were directed as much at the Kabaka as at the Europeans. Here, there was no focus of African power like the Kabaka. Not as far as anyone knew.

They overspent, of course, and were glad to be on the train coming back, with sunburn lotion and sandwiches because, they pretended, it was hard to cope with the kids in the dining-car. Then a day keeping them occupied in Nairobi until midnight arrival in Nakuru, where they had left the car in somebody's garden and Ellen had to wait with the children, sleepy and grizzling, till Jack fetched it. Perhaps it was a mistake not to have taken the ayah along, but it all cost money, and they had little enough time otherwise to spend with the children.

To be honest, she preferred Nairobi for a change. The weather was less extreme, the museum growing; there were cinemas, lovely shops, now and again a live stage show. You might afford a cup of tea at the Norfork and get a glimpse of London fashion, allowing for a timelag. In Nairobi you met people who were not tied to the land, civil servants and teachers who expected home leave and retirement, businessmen and lawyers and doctors who could move house if it suited them.

Ellen was still making her London suits and felt hats do for school. Imported material was in short supply during the war, so she had some blouses and tent-like maternity dresses run up out of Indian cotton. Fortunately she had never set her heart on dress as much as Beatrice had. Mummy used to say, "Manners may make a man but clothes make a lady." The three girls had sometimes cringed at her fixed ideas of what was suitable for each occasion, but at least there had been a yardstick which you did not seem to have any more.

In any case, while Jack was away she had not been able to have the trips to Nairobi, let alone new clothes. The

84

Mistris had once offered her a lift down, with Nigel, but it was awkward with Indians, not being able to take them out for a meal or stay in the same place, so she refused and they never offered again. In any case, she had never stayed in a hotel by herself, let alone with a baby.

A new crop of soldier-settlers was now arriving, men who were restless after war service in tropical places, their womenfolk brilliantly made up with hair aggressively free of the service caps and bandannas of recent years. Their clothes were skimpy and their eyes popped out of their heads when you asked them over, from the rudimentary training quarters in the Egerton Agricultural School, to a simple supper of ham and eggs or roast chicken. Fresh fruit salad sent them into ecstasy.

They were a strange lot – shopwalkers who had got commissions in the army, former law students who could not bear to return to the grind, and quartermasters who had no civilian job to go back to. Some of the women had been land girls, not afraid of hard work but inexperienced in planning. Some were new marriages, masking painful memories, seeking a fresh start.

Ellen saw herself a few years back, goggling at mouse-birds, sentimental over monkeys. She answered a host of questions and fielded many more, smiling inwardly to think that she also had once expected to know about big game safari gear and cocktails on exotic terraces. Well, perhaps not expected but not ruthlessly ruled out the thought. Jack discoursed learnedly on yields and acreages, cereal pests and predators. If the guests could not take that in, they had better think again. Some of them would make it, as uncle had. She handed round his photograph from the bureau drawer, smiling broadly in jodhpurs and a wide-brimmed hat, Emily tight-lipped beside him in her buttoned-up blouse and straw boater.

Back at school, Ellen managed to keep her life ticking over to a known rhythm: it was not what she had expected, but it worked. Mrs. Banerjee was now full-time and over-joyed to think her children would be able to complete their education from home. Ellen would have wished the same, but there were not so many European schools so it was no good showing envy.

The dream of secondary classes in future hovered before all the teachers. Costs were going up everywhere, but the Asian community guaranteed to get the building done within the estimates, and they did so. Ellen felt very proud. You had to be careful to use the title Asian, because some of them had links wiht the new country, Pakistan. They were enlarged. she saw. by freedom in India and Pakistan. And sensed, if she did not see, another kind of complicity, Asian offices let cheap to Kikuyu businessmen, printed books and notices in that language finding their way to the backstreet shops, children from the Babu schools eager to air their knowledge of African languarges and chatter on the streets with people from the areas where they traded.

Two thousand Kikuyu women cmae to the DC's office in Fort Hall to complain about terracing. Ellen thought it was magnificent. Why should they be sent out to work when they ought to be looking after their homes and babies? And gardens: she conceded that much.

She could picture them, wiry, short women with prominent features and wide range of skin colour, one shoulder bared under the cloth (dyed yellow with Brooke Bond tea packets as like as not), rings massed round the head on strings, ears fantastically looped, the crowns of the olders ones shaved and shiny to show (Njoki had told her)

86

that they had married children and were of an age to give counsel. The strap of the *ciondo* had bitten into their foreheads and, the *bossa Kikiyu* (Sister O'Brien explained), a protuberance low on the constantly bent back, made child-birth hard for them. They lifted loads no man on the farm could equal. And they had come together.

She spoke about it to the ayah, she did not now remember which one, but the girl had looked very severe.

"They are bad women, madam, going against the government."

"That's a revolution, all right," said Jack. "It won't make the D. C. change his mind but it will give their husbands a thing or two to think about."

She dared to mention it in class.

"It is the influence of Mr. Gandhi," someone said. "You see, the women helped to free India."

"This country," remarked Premchand, a stocky, literal-minded boy, "will also become free."

Nonetheless, the women were made to plant grass.

Chapter 5

On Tuesdays and Fridays the young man who helped at the grocery store checked the post for them in Nakuru. Ellen did not have much cause to register the days of the week, but she always woke up knowing when it was a post day, as certainly as when you had a baby you woke at its slightest whimper. And in the wartime, when she had babies, she was also avid for the overseas mail.

Even after the war, her parents' letters were brave but bleak. At home they were lucky, they said, but much of Britain was a land of prefabs and bed-sitters. The post-war baby boom was understandable, and it was marvelous that the children had cheap milk and National Health care, but their own morale sounded very low. Of course, age and the loss of Stanley had pulled them down, and so did the long period of risk and austerity they were not used to. They wondered about the future for Beatrice and Colin now that India was independent. Mavis' husband could still not get enough groceries to sell, and Mavis had to help in the shop when the children were in school.

Ellen dared raise the question of going on a visit. It was ten years since she had seen the family: if they left it too late to introduce the children they would never forgive themselves. Really, there was more to it than that, though she did not know how to make Jack see it. Mrs. Smith inhabited the same body as Miss Mountford, still wore some of her old clothes, recited in her head the same recollected poetry, but there the conjunction ceased. All her new experience, incarnate in the robust, masterful children, was remote from her family. The food she ate, the neutral utensils with which she operated in Uncle's home, the reverential gulf between herself and her students, the jargon of the farm and the casual profanity of the Club were like a blackout curtain blocking off the shared sky. And the woodsmoke, the glowing charcoal, the rutted roads on her side of the curtain must be more than matched by incendiary bombs and craters on the other.

Jack was sympathetic. He did not remind the children that there were few people to see of the Smith side. They were already muddled about the varying lengths of day and night. To teach them that things must be more respected because they were old than because they were new was beyond him. There had been some war bonus, he said. If Ellen took a term off school, they would be able to manage. It had better be the June term because there were no public exams and also you would not need warm clothes for summer in England. She winced at the thought of the clothes they had: then it struck her that England might be worse. How much worse, she had yet to find out.

They sailed in April and Jack came-down to see them off, too busy with the arrangements to analyse the restlessness all around. He marshalled them aboard, at his best when in command. The Castle boat was shabby compared to that first time, or perhaps it was Ellen's eye that was jaded, but the children were crazy with excitement. She had never meant them to be ayah's children but in fact was not used to having them full-time on her hands. She dared not let them out of her sight and was afraid they would disturb the two ladies with whom they shared the cabin. She tried to explain what they were seeing – the Suez Canal, Alexandria, Genoa. They dared not wander far on the shore stops and could not afford the package trips. Only at Gibraltar, the last port of call, they managed a ride in a horse carriage.

London River at last. Ellen found herself weeping with excitement at the grey, smelly water, the dingy wharves and terrace houses. A few of the bomb sites were filled with new blocks of flats or coloured factory buildings. Others remained desolate, without even the enormous advertisement hoardings of the old bays. She was no longer moved by the memory of that emotion. Anything she might now wish for outside her immediate surroundings came from a longer perspective, as an East African hominid might once have been dazzled by the ice-bound expanse of the animal north. Even Angela did not write from England about the pageantry of history but about the gadgetry of a breast-cancer clinic. It was as though she had lost sight of Angela as a living person too.

The children were thrilled and puzzled by the docks, customs and the train to London. There, at the arrival platform, was Father, upright, smiling, terribly thin. Mother sat behind, prim, puzzled, obviously not seeing them. Ellen dared not let go of the children or lose sight of the porter with her three suitcases, but somehow the meeting was made. The children hung back, shy of their grannie and her extended arms. A stout woman, loud-voiced, from somewhere behind, shouted, "Ellen, that's all of you!"

"Mavis!"

"Just got a parking, dear, left of the main gate. Is that all your luggage? Let me see to it while you bring the old dears. You can see they're a bit done up. Take your time."

Of course she had seen pictures of London streets, but devastation going on mile after a mile, that was a shock. Then a bit of country road, then home, not much changed but looking small in the grey air.

"You niggly Nigel," said Mavis, mock severe. "I'll bring two boys to see you later on, tough boys like me. You have
90

to mind your Ps and Qs with them. I couldn't squeeze us all into the car this morning. Besides we all thought you'd bring a couple of hippos and a chimpanzee with you. Where would we have put them?"

The parents fussed and made do, not very well fed even now. "We are all right," they said, "but it is hard on young couples starting up, or those who were bombed out; only plain white china and export reject materials: it has to go to export, you see, to pay for what we used and bust up. You are well out of it. Tell us about the house, the farm, the school, the shops. Have you *really* never seen a lion or an elephant? You aren't just trying to ease our minds?"

She worried about her parents, but perhaps even in peacetime one would be shocked by change after ten years. Their demands on life had dwindled: perhaps they were content. Mavis, Roy and the two boys were, close at hand and helpful: many things were still rationed, but at least Mavis could bring the order over from the shop and be the first to know of any coupon-free treat on the market. They no longer had to eat whalemeat or pea pods or nourishing Woolten pie made of potatoes.

Béatrice, of course, had come home after Partition and learned how to do her own cooking and washing, but she took it hard. Colin had a dull job at London Airport and, long before retirement age, he started living on his memories. They pretended that the children needed a British education, but they were not really all that bright. All the same it might be a good thing that their grand manners should be undermined before it was too late. The parents would go over at weekends sometimes and Mother and Beatrice would relax in rosy anecdotes of the memsahib's life and plaintive admiration of the Benares ware and the carpets.

Clothes were still rationed, so Ellen need not confess that she could not afford to buy much. Beatrice presented her with a garden party dress of figured cotton from India which she altered to New Look length. Consequently, she felt half naked in her old knee-length skirts. Mother still looked neat, regardless of fashion, in clothes that would have been called "dressy" ten years before. ("After all, look at the dear queen, always the same.")

New books came printed on grey wartime paper, splotched with bits of stem and leaf, all except the very latest. So Ellen stocked up with second-hand ones. You could find them for six pence or a shilling outside the shabbier bookshops round Charing Cross Road or close to the precincts of Cathedral cities. Father insisted that the children must see these historic places, and for her they were a breath of fresh air. Nigel was old enough to know that to have seen the royal palaces and the changing of the guard would give him credit with his school-fellows later on. What they really enjoyed was the seaside, with brass bands playing and sticks of rock. The piers were still truncated for fear of invasion and the ornamental railings had not been replaced since they were melted down for munitions. The sunshine seemed not as bright as it had once been. There were still jam tarts of a unique glazed sweetness at Lyons' tea shops, and the same uncles and aunts she remembered broadcasting on the children's hour. They were a bit too prim and proper for Nigel.

They visited relations and a few shrines of personal memory. The old school was rising from the devastation, some classes going on in Nissen huts borrowed from the service till repairs were finished. The Ashtons' was spick and span now that war damage people had done their work. Margaret Ashton had gone to Kansas as a G.I. bride. One night Ellen left the children with Mavis so that she could stay over and see a play Lily had a small part in.

Lily was a shock. One could still recognise her intelligence, her vivacity and her toughness. But the plasticity learned from stage training – transformation by role, costume and make-up, whether in the theatre or outside – dazzled and disturbed. There was a husband somewhere, but he did not figure in the conversation, posed no limit to ambition. Lily was battering on the doors of Ealing Studies. Ellen felt threatened as by a presence from another planet. Or was that only in recollection?

On safer ground, they must report on Mrs. Galsworthy, who flourished. She had found a job as cashier in a department store and a flat in an old-fashioned house now profitably partitioned into four. Perhaps getting control, at last, of a separate kitchen had brought out a new confidence in her. The boy and girl exulted in outdoor play during the long summer evenings, buying attention from the other kids with fictioned reminiscences of lion and hippopotamus. Ellen watched for signs that Nigel and Angela might envy them, and saw none.

Father talked obliquely of fuel shortages in the winter and electricity cuts; they had an oil heater for emergency and a haybox for slow cooking. The children longed for snow and skating.

"It's like meat and drink to Mother to see you all. I so much hope Jack is going to make it."

She knew in her bones that she had never expected him to make it. He was needed on the farm. Surely to goodness they could see that Kenya was not a land of milk and honey to which only the export products were flowing. But their sense of comparison had been dulled by the streams of refugees and the images of those who were never going to return. To travel from a home intact, to have fresh fruit and meat every day (even in the midst of other people wizened by drought), to have ones's small skills made much of, seemed satisfactory to them. Looking back, one began to see why.

Ellen was not sorry to leave behind so tenuous a reflection of another life, chilly, grudging of service. She was not renewed (as she had expected) by the mere sight of great monuments and pictures, as the elders shrank and the world policy reversed itself. Teachers in the new Britain had not yet got their cars back and would not be the first to do so.

"It will be better, mind you," Mavis insisted, "more people able to eat decently instead of a few feasting from Fortnum and Mason's. Next time you come you'll see people riding in cars who never had a bike before, and getting their new teeth and glasses on the National Health without giving it a second thought."

But there had never been a next time.

The boat journey confirmed a certainty: this was Mrs. Smith going home. The liner was still crowded and not smart enough to demean her. The fancy dress part was subdued: Nigel caught nobody's eye in a cotton shirt and a fez, Angela made a despondent Miss Muffet. Ellen, with a circlet on her hair and a wand, called herself Circe: nobody had ever heard of Circe.

They came back to a world that related by time-shift to an older Europe that had had the stuffing knocked out of it. In Kenya you still made steak and kidney pudding and used three eggs in a cake. The children were taught to dance round a maypole and trace outlines of an Empire on which the sun never set. Only their grandfather, perhaps, could apprehend the ironic present and anticipate its passing.

94

Still, like those millions more forcibly displaced, you got along with things as they were. You would scour Whiteaways or the Emporium for something fit to wear, according to the fashion drawings in the *East African Standard*, that could be copied by a Goan tailor in Nakuru. The last detachable collar dropped from the last of Jack's pre-war shirts. Ladies' vests vanished and one could get by with a suspender belt instead of the oppressive foundation garments of earlier days. But the time had not yet come when one could walk bare-legged into the classroom. Only ballet dancers had heard of tights. Nylon swept into the country, so widespread that Africans named the new flu virus after it.

Honeymoon frocks were only fished out for weddings of big-busted Kenya whites or Empire Day receptions: most of the gauzy dresses had long since been cut up for baby clothes. The last of the floppy hats did duty when the Queen Mother and Princess Margaret came out in 1956. You were still expected to wear a hat for formal occasions and a kind of straw sombrero round the farm. The old winter felts from London still came in useful: the crazy angles of the war days had come and gone. You might feel like Bette Davies twenty years on, but the titled ladies were looking much the same.

Within a few days of their return, Ellen was back on duty. She took the daily grind for granted and did not look much better for her holiday, people said. In some ways she felt more at home than before, knowing now that she was a stranger in Britain, schooled in austerity of a kind but not initiated with the rest into wartime experience. The children drove into town every day with her, but next year Nigel would be going to Nairobi Primary School as a boarder.

Jack was more talkative than usual, happy to see them back. He was not very curious about London. He had spent his time chewing over the squatter problem, as the powers that be defined it, with his friends, bargaining over his labour, coming to terms with the new soldier settlers. They thought they were getting a favour from the Empire they had defended: in fact, of course, they had been brought out not to feed their own ambitions but to keep the cattle healthy, which was as much as to say to keep the white highlands white.

The Smith farm was run with regular, paid labour, so although the workers had gardens they were not defined as squatters. All the same, Ellen noticed, the few cows they used to keep had vanished and more sheep had been brought in instead. This was the bargain Jack had made with the staff. Everyone was terrified of foot-and-mouth disease, and government pressure was heavy.

She sensed a closing up of faces that had once been open to her, an evasiveness when she admired the standing crops or vegetables on sale. Kirui said it was because people were unhappy at having had to send their cows to the reserve. She could understand how they felt. But rules were rules. Some invisible legal force had divided the land, and everybody told her there was plenty of room in the reserve for those who wanted to go there.

When the newspapers declared that the new influx of agricultural and veterinary officers was improving life in the reserve, she did not see this as a cause for resentment in the present or a threat to her livelihood in the future. But other people did. And that women's revolt, Jack said, had been flying in the face of improvement.

It was all very well to restrict people's rights for their own good, she supposed. Every school took for granted the power to do that. (Would the system really collapse if you got your hair permed or wore high-heeled shoes or helped your mother on Saturdays instead of playing in the hockey match?) Mummy's daily woman used to tell her about her young days as a housemaid, living in, where the rule was "no followers". That meant your boyfriend was not allowed to call for you even in your time off. But, she said, supposing you really kept the rule and never left to get married? Would the lady still be there to employ you when you were forty and on the shelf?

Jack told her to keep her mouth shut about all that in public, or it would be impossible for him to hire a tractor or get his subsidies approved. It was one thing for old Josh and Nellie Grant to be eccentric, he said, with all their years of seniority, and not enough success for anyone to envy. Not the same thing at all if you were a latecomer, with children to consider. She took the point.

She wondered about life in India, and what had happened to all the family retainers when so many Europeans left, some after generations. Her girls were so good at everything pretty and graceful. They put on splendid dances while some grave elderly person played the sitar or changed the gramophone records. They carried milk or flowers to the temple. Yet Beatrice never spoke of any of these things. She seemed quite cut off from them.

Ellen understood that she also was cut off from African life. There was a slow growth of understanding but no epiphany. She had never been invited to house in the African part of the town. Once or twice she had watched Sunday dances among the Wakamba on the big farms, with whistles blowing and seemingly inexhaustible figures leaping up and down. But the other staff held aloof. She had visited

Njoroge's mother when she came to stay, a bright-eyed little lady but they had no language in common.

After careful thought Ellen took her some sugar, which turned out to be the right thing to do, though in England it would have been horribly patronising. Wilberforce, who was learning to play the cornet, had asked her to go to Salvation Army rally, but she was hesitant about taking the children.

She had twice talked to the church elder who visited the staff quarters and asked him why the government did not set up a school for all the children of different farms. Few land-owners could afford to do so even if they were willing, and the smaller farms like their own would not fill up even one classroom. The teacher explained that there was no land nearby to set up African facilities: people must send their children either to the township or to the reserve if they wanted to educate them, and most could not afford to do so. The reserve, he said, was ten years ahead of the settlement area in such things. Why then, she wondered, did the people leave it? Because of land shortage, cash money, family squabbles... Neither his English nor her Swahili was adequate for a real explanation. Njoroge had sent his sons away to school, but taught the daughters to read and write at home. They had to read the bible, he insisted. Kimalel shook his head and said there were no schools near his home place. Ellen was puzzled but did not have much time to think about it. In 1951 they were starting secondary classes, and some of the Indian girls were allowed to stay on, though some families thought this too dangerous. Their good name might be endangered, even (perhaps it was obscurely felt) the matriarchal discipline of the home. Mwangi believed – was it possible? – that his daughter would be attending an Indian school. (They learned to say Asian, now that India had changed its shape on the map.)

But Mwangi was not there to see the expansion. He had vanished from Mr. Galsworthy's office some time in 1950, into detention. (Mau Mau was proscribed the same year, two years before the declaration of Emergency. Until then they had been told there was no such thing as Mau Mau.)

"They always take the clever ones," Mr, Galsworthy grumbled.

"Goodness knows what he's supposed to have done. I have no complaint about him. Did his work well and polite to everybody."

"Perhaps it's harder for that sort to accept the kind of regulations . . ."

"Live and let live, I say. But of course you farmers . . ."

"The land is in bad heart. Look at that report . . ."

"True enough, I daresay. But unhappy people do not work for a good heart. Have you ever been to Ireland?"

No, she had not. Ireland was beyond her imagination. Kenya as a whole was beyond her imagination too: she had seen so little of it. Of course, the workers ought to have more money. She remembered that every time, she went to the rondavels to welcome a new baby or encourage a bright child to read. The church elder used to teach them to read by lamplight after work, but now any meeting by lamplight was suspect. She had bought them an ABC and a number chart and a few slates and some chalk, but she did not talk to Jack about it. She had once met the lady from Ulu buying, in a Nairobi bookshop, pictures and friezes, full of enthusiasm for her school.

"She will be sorry for it," one of the other farmers prophesied shaking his head. Ellen remembered reading about

Sunday schools in the England of child employment, teaching not so much bible knowledge as the three Rs to children who, at seven or eight, would be sucked away into working life. Yet if the people were to get enough for school fees and uniforms, where could it come from except her teacher's salary? The bank swallowed up the farm income: what was wrong?

"Give these Kikuyu an inch," said Jack, "and they'll take an ell. Like they set up their own independent schools, make out they're poor, then they start *schools* for goodness sake. If you're not careful they'll be setting up banks, clubs, swimming-pools."

He was getting red in the face again. She ought to give it a rest. But there is no rest if the acrid smoke of misapprehension prevents your seeing one another clearly. She made a mental note to look up the length of an ell before the next proverbs and sayings lesson. The Chief Education Officer, she remembered, had attended the opening of the Independent Teachers' College at Githunguri, with Colonel and Mrs. Lafontaine. Was that not enough to make it respectable? ("Oh, Mrs. *Laff*," hissed the ladies, "ready to address any black man as *Bwana*. Really, how soft can you get?")

"But *we* set up private schools, those who can afford it and are not satisfied with the government system. So why should they not do the same? And what a lovely idea to have a Kikuyu bank, so that people need not feel embarrassed by strangers looking over their shoulder if the deposit is small or if they have to use a thumb-print. Why should they *want* to be like us?"

Jack growled. That was enough for the day.

She supposed the separate land units were meant to make it easier for people – separate school, separate hous-
100

ing locations, separate entrances in some shops. And yet when she used to study the *Gazette*, back in the war days, to find out about controlled prices and scheduled crops, she had been surprised to find out how much was *not* differentiated – notices of bankruptcy, court cases, probate, all in one list, regardless of race, and no doubt charged at the same rate. Even contributions to war charities were gazetted – ten shillings was a lot for an African worker to give. So why not one staff list, one ration card?

And where did you find them, these Africans who owned bus companies and sued one another? Did those teachers you met in Nakuru make wills and change their names by deed poll? It was not something you could ask them at the Boy Scout rally or in the bookshop. That would be rude. You could only ask how many pupils had passed for intermediate or how they were getting on with their correspondence courses.

Back home things were not so cut and dried, but Mother had very clear ideas about what was *common*, not suitable for her daughters. Lily's father would not, she supposed, have a bank account: maybe a few shares in the Coop if he were lucky. Annie Beach would not visit the West End shops unless defiantly, on principle. No railway clerk would ask her which class she wanted to travel. But Lily now, saved by the bell and the Beveridge Report. What were you going to exclude Lily from? Her father had been gassed defending a dream of a land fit for heroes to live in. And little Marian? What sort of country did her father think he was sweating for, digging ditches, sullen-faced, according to the newspaper photographs, surrounded by watchtowers and weaponry, turning silent backs to earnest evangelists, being graded according to the ferocity of his perceived convictions?

Now, after the years of frantic rehabilitation, turning your back on wartime horrors, cossetting Jewish orphans into English diphthongs and Sunday teas, finding work for bereaved Czech airmen and Polish sappers, submerging memories of far eastern prison camps in Earling Studio movies and Butlins holidays – the true stories were beginning to come out and get attention. One found the prisoner of war enclosures had been hives of busy escapers. Resistance networks had been political coalitions of amateurs juggling with death: information networks had papered over the holocaust and the squabbles of allies.

Would it ever be so with this minor, close-at-hand conflict, where the smooth-skinned identified themselves as Baganda, the squatters of the empty plain laid claim to secret jungle knowledge, the poker-faced accepted vacant jobs and houses, never acknowledging what secret tribute of cash and sympathy might be being paid?

She wondered, but knew she did not know. Some never wondered but were sure they knew. Some winced and kept the country going. Some pleaded the necessity of better education and ran.

"You must have been young when you lost your husband," Ellen asked suddenly. "I wish I had known you then, Martha. Those were bad times for your people."

"I was twenty-seven, madam, I had had five children, but two died before him. It was hard enough, but the Lord has helped me and shown me how to help myself."

Njogu had not been bad to her. He worked as a driver and would come and go, come and go, while the children were little, until one day he came no more. It was not a time for asking questions, but word was brought that he had been dragged out of the truck and despatched at the forest edge, in case he might tell where the iron pipes and the bat-
102

tery had gone to. Soon they were moved from the little wooden house to the new village, carrying what planks and struts they could. Njogu had been, of course, older than her, his parents already dead, his sisters-in-law at once loud and secretive: she had to do what she could, digging, taking in laundry for the men who had avoided detention, urging the children to their lessons.

The message might not be true, but she did not think Njogu went to the forest – he would have been more useful on the road – or into the camp: the news would have got out sooner or later.

He had never told her much and no one came to question her. In the town, people said, there were women: the sisters-in-law implied that others would know more than herself.

One of Njogu's brothers they knew to be detained. He was one of the first to be released, moved on and prospered: they did not ask how he had managed to get a share in a timber business. The other sent for his wife – at least that is what she said when she went away with the assent of the guards. They did not know where.

Martha's mother had died by then and the younger children scattered among relations. Her father's employers retired to the coast and took him with them: she was delighted, it was the best thing that could happen to keep him safe. Once or twice she received money from him for school fees when someone was coming on leave: probably he sent messages more often than, in those risky times, she received them. He died eventually in hospital and it was quite a long time before she got the news.

Gradually the restrictions grew less, the villages cracked open though the old homesteads still lay silent, mudded floors palpable beneath the grass. New learning was opening to young people, even to girls, and Lilian did well at school. Njogu was scarcely remembered; one must, somehow, seize for the children what the future offered.

That bright spot – like those old tin advertisements for Stephen's ink – must be a sweet paper blown in from the road, the colour of a blue bag. How many years since she had used one? She remembered her father prodding with a stick, boiling his master's sheets in a brick furnace which for some reason was called a copper, the stewed cabbage smell, the steam rising, the blue giving a sheen to the white linen like snow on the mountain top seen from below. You were not expected to boil any more unless you had a twin-tub such as she had seen in Mrs. Banerjee's kitchen. And there were no more plain white sheets. But in those laundry days she had always kept a bit of blue about . . . First in the new village, scrubbing away after that long walk to the fields and back . . . Then more washing at the road junction which had started to become a trading centre and was now a little a town – her fingers still tingled with it, white shirt for the clerks, tablecloths and chair-backs for the teachers, white coats for the medical assistants.

"They could use you," one of them said, "in Nakuru Hospital." So she made the journey, battered on doors, transferred the children to new schools, set them to work on a little plot beside the railway line, while Lilian did her intermediate and William his standard three and four (two having died between). Stephen by this time had finished his standard eight and gone to Mombasa to stay with an uncle and find work, but he stopped writing and it was thought he had gone away on a boat . . .

In Nakuru Hospital they paid regular money: here she had seen sterilisers and here again they boiled the sheets to get rid of nameless horrors, and put them back on beds

104

where people had died: (even Kikuyu people who had been taught that you polluted a whole building by dying inside it).

They did not bother with the blue there, but even now she shuddered to remember the pads and napkins. *Here, under the hedge, were the pink indigestible innards of some rat, spit out by a passing cat, no doubt, and how could the new mothers bear the touch?. . .*

The whole history of blood, long since dried, came to mind, how significantly it begins and yet is soon taken for granted, punctuates the progress to wifehood, motherhood, widowhood, and then one day ceases and you are glad to be shot of it and all the bother. At least if it happens naturally – perhaps if they cut it out of you you would feel deprived. You do not even celebrate the new cleanness and temporary discomfort, but seal up your lips as though you had never passed through the muggy, productive mist into the lucid tableland above. How should sterilisation be so steamy, smelling of chemicals and waste, when to be sterile should be light and dry and powerful (no more oaths or tea-drinking, no banana arches)? But power has its limits, blind spots. The children had gone beyond her reach and the old one whom she nursed like a child was going too.

She had never talked with anyone about these things: nowadays the young talk about anything, forget that they are women, do not even take the time to get over childbirth properly. They put little self-dissolving stitches into you so that the doctor or the midwife does not even have to look. In the political world also the blood had (more or less) ceased to flow, but no one looked to see if there was a clean scar or matter festering inside the closed-off place.

Chapter 6

"Who was that at the door, Martha?"

"Just Tallboy from the grocery store. I suppose he must have a proper name but he likes to be called Tallboy. He says Councillor Mwangi sent this newspaper for you."

"Newspaper? I can't hold up a newspaper properly."

"He knows that, so let me see why . . . Oh yes, here is a passage marked in ink: 'Narendra V. Shah (picture left) is honoured by becoming the new chairman of the Nakuru Businessmen's Charitable Trust. Mr. Shah was one of the first batch of students to join form I in Nakuru in 1951, and he would like the Trust to set up a scholarship each year for a student who gains admission to the school but cannot meet the fees,"

"Narendra? Oh what good news."

Ellen felt proud. She remembered her skills coming back with the senior group, those who had passed Kenya's equivalent of the scholarship. Alas, that did not mean a free place! It was the end of school for those who could not find the fees, and parents of Indian girls, of course, must always remember they had dowry to provide.

The children from her own primary school had some command of English: if they were not correct, they had at least, some deviant notion of correctness. It was those bred in country *dukas*, who had got their schooling, in a mixture of ages, abilities and home languages, from a *Babu* hired hopefully from the community, who came in with their weird private vocabulary and phonetic spelling or, all too often, could not communicate their need to come in at all. *Wikel* was vehicle, which they preferred to car or bus, *demise* was death, *departure* was separation. Some of them dropped out early, proud to be seen driving huge haulage

106

vehicles or commanding gangs of porters. Others hung on with unfailing optimism till exam time, professing in tortured sentences an ambition towards medicine or the law. But most worked compulsively, imitated with precision whatever models the school chose to set before them, qualified at Cambridge Overseas level for the intricacies of business. A few with money and grit achieved the professional qualifications they all aspired to.

"Madam, why does Mark Anthony call being ambitious a grievous fault? We are all urged to be ambitious."

"Why was Mr. Bennet displeased at Elizabeth receiving an advantageous proposal from a clergyman?"

"Why does he say 'not half' when he means 'very'?"

In the classroom a variant speech had to be standardised – as Lily's had been – if possible without losing its piquancy. An erratic reading of a text had to be checked. An enthusiasm had to be stimulated that would go beyond the desire for good marks. At the elocution contest they all tended to read as though they had a train to catch. They seemed to like *Westward Ho! The History of Mr. Polly* struck them as vulgar. Even those who seemed slow were not facing you with defiance but with a carefully structured differentness screened by other knowledge – wide polished verandahs, strange gestures and high pitched voices.

School, Jack said, must not take her mind off reality. Nigel was getting ready to move up to secondary at the Prince of Wales School. They had to decide whether Angela should also go away to complete her primary education: for secondary she would certainly have to. Ellen dreaded the thought, but she also feared the increasingly uneasy atmosphere round her. They decided to send Angela to Loreto Convent when she was old enough to start standard four.

Having been away, Ellen was more conscious than Jack of grey resentment in the air. The men were more sullen, the children more often away. Small items began to disappear: she told herself it was natural for the men to want more things as they got used to seeing teapots and table-cloths in clerks' houses, teachers wearing ties and socks. But that was not it. Some pressure was acting on them from outside. They were glad to get the telephone connected while Mau Mau was hardly more than a nip in the air. Then came the city strikes: you could not blame skilled men for bargaining, but there were reports of intimidation and some officials had very casual views about what subsistence meant. Nairobi was getting its charter as a city. And Italy was getting Somalia back. Ellen remembered what Joe Holmes had said. It was not Ethiopia yet, but how long could the big Nations go on doing deals in the smaller ones? British India was free but Goa not. Her students educated her on the implications.

They took more and more of her attention, especially after Angela went away to school. Jack was drinking more, not spectacularly but spending a lot of time with neighbouring farmers and Nakuru businessmen, swaggering with a holster at the hip and bragging about what they would do if they caught any Mau Mau interfering with their property. The pistols and the bravado did not do much to endear him to the labourers who remained on the farm after Kamau and Mwangi had been taken away to detention, but, to do him justice, he never bullied them individually or showed fear of them. A couple of cows were slaughtered and removed and the spare wheel and headlamps were taken from the old Ford standing outside a neighbour's place in the evening. At last they had sufficient excuse to trade it in for a more recent model. That was all you could count, though necessarily there was a trickle of stores and less ponderable items – observation, use of rooms and implements, and movement of children.

Ellen carried a pepperpot wherever she went, and sometime a long thin whip that was supposed to be for tripping assailants up, but never a gun. Guns were what the fighters wanted most and the hope of stealing one might, she believed, provoke an attack. She taught the children to be polite to everybody alike, which caused some embarrassment when they were visiting school friends. The Emergency went on round them but it did not consume them.

In 1952 Kirui expressed a wish to retire. This had something to do with an inheritance in his home village, he said, and recommended a protege of his called Muoki. It did not for a long time occur to the Smiths that political pressures might be weighing on Kirui too. They missed him but did not feel it right to press him to stay.

Mutua performed adequately his duties of cooking and cleaning. He was not an aspiring member of the household, but not focus of suspicion either. He spent most of his spare time in the quarters: now that there was no need of ayahs he could have both rooms if he liked, but he shunned the society of the farm workers and never brought his family to visit. Mutua had left home in Machakos during the 1994 famine and got outdoor work at a neighbouring farm. Kirui took him under his wing and taught him some of his own skills. Mutua resented having to work away from home and had no intention of mixing up the two sides of his life. He did not talk readily about his wife and children, and Ellen could only guess at which of the outgrown clothes would be of service to him when he went on leave. When she occasionally checked the empty room she found a carton tied up with string and some bunches of herbs hanging from the ceiling. She felt no desire to investigate further. Closed rooms came naturally to her.

Each holiday, Nigel and Angela came home a little more remote from her, critical and demanding. They were no great readers or letter-writers. They were civil to the staff, aware, though impatient, of precautions required in Emergency times. Their school reports were tolerable and they had no intention of discussing them. Jack was not perturbed by this. She was the teacher, he implied, and supposed to know what was what. He had enough to think about with foot and mouth disease only ten miles away. Beatrice's children and Mavis's seemed to have blundered into adulthood and found themselves occupation away from home. One should not have to worry. There were plenty of jobs for white youngsters in Kenya but the lines of demarcation were changing. It was no longer enough to be able to express yourself in kitchen Swahili and apply the manipulative skills that come from practice with mechanical toys and spatial puzzles. The Coronation Safari was enough to demonstrate that. It put East Africa on the sporting map of the world and provided a focus of enthusiasm for all the men and boys who thought they had nothing better to do at Easter time. Jack and Nigel sat glued to the radio, checking off points on their score-cards, and waited patiently for hours by the roadside. But although in the first years Kenya resident drivers dominated the event, those from other countries soon came into their own. And so would those whose local knowledge was absolute but not yet recognised by the motor manufacturers.

Father had been right: the war had helped people get used to changes. Even so, Mummy was never happy about Mavis serving in the shop. During the war, of course,

110

everyone had to do his bit, but afterwards she felt it a comedown, so was hardly sorry when, in 1955, Roy and his brother sold out to the inevitable supermarket chain and invested in a small seaside hotel.

Martha brought out the morning tea. She could get the floors done while Mrs. Smith sat outside, but she got dreamy if she was too long alone.

"Tallboy says there was an accident down at the corner yesterday", said Martha loudly. "One of the young men decided to try his hand at the tractor, drove it into the hedge and nearly tipped over."

Mrs. Smith appeared not to hear, but in fact the story reactivated her memories. In 1956 Jack had an accident with a tractor he had hired from a bigger farm. (Uncle's old one had long since given out.) He had been driving it back with Wilberforce, who succeeded Kamau, when it heeled over in the rutted track, throwing them both into a prickly hedge. Jack had his left arm jammed in the machinery. Wilberforce was just a bit scratched and had a sprained ankle: he was able to call for help, and the men who came extricated Jack and then righted the tractor. His lower arm was lacerated and fractured, the right shoulder dislocated, where Wilberforce had fallen on him or else with the clumsy effort used to pull him out. A couple of ribs were cracked.

Of course people said it was no accident. The Mau Mau must have fixed it some way. Ellen didn't believe a word of it. No one had offered violence or touched the gun: the tractor was not out of action for long. Jack had had a few beers at lunch, and was in any case getting careless: she was not keen on driving with him any more. Foul words came to him easily if he fumbled with the gear lever or slopped water out of the spare can. He was not used to the width of the tractor, and the road was hardly better than it had been when she first arrived.

Called out of school by telephone, she found him being brought into the War Memorial Hospital as she arrived. He was walking but redfaced, dishevelled, badly shaken. Impersonally she was sorry for his hurt, his humiliation, the fear of future disability that haunted them both. She winced as the doctor bared, swabbed, probed, but this was a pity for the process, the reduction of human contact to technicalities. It was no longer flesh of her flesh and dutiful service was all it could command.

Mr. Galsworthy laid a steadying hand on her arm, but it had never been steadier. She saw it now and was glad of the clarity of the vision. She could cope. She could drive herself home. No, she did not need company. The children would be breaking up from school in a day or two. After she had been served with the usual tough chicken and vegetables, she unlocked the inner larder and opened a packet of chocolate biscuits, meant for the children's homecoming, to have with her coffee. There would be hospital expenses – the local contributory scheme could no longer cover everything – and perhaps they would need extra help on the farm while Jack convalesced. They would pay for repairing the tractor and – she decided at once – a hundred shillings for Wilberforce, a bottle of whisky for the farmer who had taken Jack to hospital and a goat for his labourers who had gone to the rescue.

But it did not end there. The farm seemed to be yielding less and less. She did not see the accounts – if indeed, there were accounts. Musa seemed to be more a storekeeper than a clerk these days – all those intricate wartime forms for target assessment and bonus claims a thing of the

112

past. There had not been a major plague, though rats and borers always did their bit in destroying stored crops. No doubt, some stores had been syphoned off to the forest: how could they not be when staff were subject to threats and appeals, let alone blood ties of those Kikuyu who remained? There had been new expenses for fencing.

She paid cash for petrol now: the main road service station said they had changed their policy, but not, she knew, for all customers. She bought the groceries in her lunch hour and sent pocket money for the children and drove down for their "outs" and bought their train tickets, to be collected by the parents on escort duty. It was only the fees Jack had to pay and the income tax and the farm expenses and the mortgage – ah, the mortgage.

They would have to talk it out, she said, when he came home. He was discharged after a fortnight, still in pain and involuntarily sober. He positively snarled at her. What interest had she ever had in the farm except as a place to sleep? He was not accountable to her for it. She had had a trip to England with the children. What had he ever spent on himself? Did she think it was child's play running an agricultural business just because grass grew by nature and cows came into calf? Uncle had already been failing when they got married. He had been a fool to put his own capital in and then go on working as unsalaried manager for the old man. Hadn't she got a furnished house out of the deal anyway, and a car?

Keeping her voice low, she acknowledged that this was so. She did not ask who else worked only for an old house and an old car. For how did one go about buying or even renting a house, furnishing it, making a new disposition of its space a personal routine? Even Mummy, sheltered as she was, would have known those things. (Mummy had

113

faded away with never a penny in her own name, but Father, conscious of that, had sent a hundred pounds in her memory for each of the children, and this Ellen guarded jealously in a separate account.)

After a tense day or two, Jack had to back down. Interest rates had gone up and they were a bit behind. He admitted that he did not have his uncle's eye for stock, and some of the purchases had not turned out well. Something, he agreed, would have to be done. But he was not like old Jos, always off to sink money into more scatter-brained schemes. Within a month he was tramping round the farm again, giving orders, though without much enthusiasm. But his arm, when the plaster came off, was still a bit out of line – no more tractor driving, no more local rallying, no more motivational displays of strength to the men. He became moody and reckless. The multiplicity of African political associations, now that the law allowed them on a local basis, provoked his scorn and his bad language.

She pondered. Perhaps it was the same as praying: at least there was a consciousness afterwards that she should say thank you. An old army friend of Jack's came to see them after he had been to a meeting in Nakuru. He was starting up an animal feed business in Kitale and looking for a storekeeper who would double as supervisor. Jack rose to it himself: she did not have to push him. After the shake-up of the accident, he said, he was finding traipsing round the farm a bit too much. And, to be honest, the animals weren't paying off as well as they had been, in spite of the Department of Agriculture being convinced they were worth subsidising. He could put in a manager for the arable if Ellen could see her way to doing without him in term-time. During the holiday she could run up to Kitale for a few days: make a change for the children. Musa could keep

114

the records on his own with a bit of supervision. Paddy jumped at it. Ellen heaved a sigh of relief.

"There are things we'll have to work out, of course, Paddy," she said, "but I haven't any objection. Basically he's fit but here he'll always be tempted to overdo it. It's not as though we were still on our honeymoon, after all. And the worst of the Emergency is over. I feel quite confident in the staff. It will help us to sort ourselves out."

He would earn less than she was getting, but no one mentioned that. There was quite a reasonable boarding house he could stay in. The sale of the cows and dairy equipment would wipe off the overdraft and go part of the way towards a second car. Would he really need a car at Kitale? Naturally, he insisted. He would be going out to see about the silage or why someone hadn't delivered on time. How would it help him to get over the accident if he had to bloody walk? She could get a lift from old Galsworthy till they were fixed up. He would need to come down at the end of every month to check on things. (She had not thought of that.) What was left from the farm income after paying the manager and staff and mortgage would be a bit of a nest-egg for the children. (What had ever been left over?)

The staff houses needed repair. The cattle man would have to go: his son, Felix, had gone to work at a garage in the town when he left the army. Maybe the Holmeses might have a job for Kimalel and be glad not to be bothered any more with the Smiths' scanty output of milk. She would give Muoki some eggs to sell for himself instead of the rise in wages he kept asking for. There would be less for him to do.

But where would the manager come from? What would he cost? Where would he live?

"You leave that to me, love; which one of us is supposed to be the farmer?"

Well, of course, he had always managed. His need for her approval had vanished the night Uncle and Kirui welcomed them home. Forty-five now, close to the change, maybe that was what was making her lose confidence. This time Jack was good as his word. Within ten days a sale was held and the place was full of pick-ups and trailers. A lot of beer was drunk and by the end of the day livestock was gone. A muscular Sikh was among those who attended: next day, swearing about the state of the track, he reappeared with three workmen and began alterations to the dairy building. A window here, an opening bricked up there, partitions, whitewash, an outdoor Elsan, a chimney: not exactly a house but a sound roof, a pitted cement floor, shutters, a few projections for fixing shelves on, an old metal sink under the existing water-tap. Mr. Thomas did not seem dismayed.

He looked absurdly young and had a pale, Arab kind of face. He was Seychellois, Jack said, and was prepared to take six hundred. He knew about machines and had experience on a fruit farm. He requested mosquito netting on the windows and transport for his things from his cousin's house in Gilgil. (The cousin had set up a home bakery there and got good custom from the army families.)

He settled in quickly and at the end of March (1957 that was) Jack drove off to Kitale. Mr. Thomas kept himself to himself. Large packets of study material came for him through the post and he must have spent most evenings working on the exercises in his small, neat writing. He had portable radio and it appeared to be company enough. There were no visitors. He seemed to get along with the men.

116

Nigel, big, fleshy and nearly seventeen, enjoyed strolling round the farm and receiving the salutes of the workers during school holidays. He had some months around the place, between visits to Kitale and school friends, before returning to Nairobi to start work as a trainee in a bank. It was he who drove the Volkswagen down from Kitale: Ellen was glad she had not known about that in advance. It was good to have him home, and yet she felt him almost a stranger, overbearing in his certainties, like a member of a tribal age-grade in which she had no place.

Where, indeed, was her place? For Father had gone, and with him all she had held to, outside herself, of dignity and order. After Mother's death, he used to potter about the house and garden, with a woman coming in to clean through once a week. He was proud of his roses and his Scotch Broth. You could still, then, find a laundry in operation and a guest-house serving a decent home-cooked Sunday lunch. They had never had central heating put in, and he used an electric fire in preference to having to haul coal about.

One winter morning, the daily woman found him collapsed in the bathroom, half dressed, freezing. They estimated he had been there for twenty four hours. In hospital he rallied for a few days but then succumbed, after sending his love to Ellen, wishing she could put a bit of sunshine in a parcel back, and teasing Colin about the old days of perspiration and empire.

Njoroge, who had passed every screening test, seemed to know what had happened and came up with his bible words of comfort. You should not grieve an old man, he said, only give thanks for him. Many people he knew had babies to mourn for, who had died of malnutrition in the reserve. Their mothers failed to give sufficient care as they

117

toiled in the fields between the curfew hours and the spells of compulsory labour. Their fathers, lost or in detention, might not even know about it. It was a comfort brought by modern ways of living to know what happened even if you could not mend it. It was good to be voting for the first time for your African MPs even if some of your Kikuyu brothers could not take part because they did not have the loyalty certificate. When your people had elders who knew and enforced the law as Mrs. Smith's departed father had done, the land would be at peace.

Does a suburban solicitor enforce the law? Ellen asked herself. At least he upholds it, nurtures his family within it. But where there is guerilla war ever the man of law forsakes his neutrality and results to subterfuge.

The Emergency somehow petered away during those years when children were growing up. Driving down to Nairobi, you noticed the home guard posts being reduced. The watch-towers in villages and boarding schools were no longer manned all round the clock. Fewer farmers swaggered with revolvers at the hip. Waves of detainees were getting released from the camps and work had to be found for them. But, technically, the Emergency was still in force.

The police came late in 1957 to arrest Muoki. Angela, mercifully, was at school in Nairobi. Nigel was at Kitale with his father. Ellen drove home from school to find Njoroge pacing about the front garden and constables digging in the copse the other side of the track.

"Muoki – what has he done?"

"No need to worry, madam," the European inspector assured her. "You won't be seeing him again. Make sure you get someone with good references next time."

118

She could not take it in, though she immediately saw how superficial her knowledge of Muoki had been. She looked pleadingly at Njoroge. For once he hung his head.

"Madam," he said in his correct Swahili that she still found a bit. hard to follow, "we have nothing to say about that man. He was not friendly to us. He would not speak about holy things. But I did not know he was a danger to you. If I know, I must tell you. But Mr. Smith trusted him."

Yes, that was it. Mr. Smith liked people to keep themselves to themselves. He never asked what might be happening outside the kitchen. Urged to check whether anything was missing, Ellen went round the house perfunctorily. She could not think of anything that had been taken. Not that that was the point.

That night she tossed and turned. She had spoken to Jack on the telephone and made herself a supper of boiled eggs and tinned beans. There was a watchman at the gate, a younger one since Mwangi had been taken away: she did not want a policeman there as well. Was it a body they were looking for? Guns? Or only the bones of a slaughtered cow? She never asked. Jack came, post-haste, asked and was not told. Nigel came back for a week or two, but Jack refused to let him have the gun: that would be asking for trouble. Stories went round the Club – it was a time bomb, a magic spell, a map of operational areas. She refused to talk about it, wrote to Angela only that Muoki had been arrested on suspicion.

Njoki, visiting her mother on the neighbouring farm she had grown up on, came back to do a little housework and washing. She was not called Njoki anymore, but Mrs. Mary Onyango, married to a watchman in Nairobi, and she worked in a soft drink factory.

Nobody supposed that she was really married to a Luo man, but you had better chance of getting a job during the Emergency if you did not have a Kikuyu name. Her real husband was still in detention. She could use the extra money and Ellen needed a few days to think things out.

Three days later Njoroge brought her a letter from Kirui and helped her to read it. Kirui was not a ready writer, and the Swahili consonants were modified by the pattern of his own speech. The gist of it was that he had heard Muoki had been removed and begged pardon for recommending such a person long before. Since Mrs. Smith had had this misfortune and he himself was eager to resume working, because one of his sons had been selected for high school and needed fees, he offered himself as a replacement. He would come and see her in two days time.

Jack saw the letter and approved the plan. He had brought an enormous turkey, already plucked, and a bag of apples. Fortunately, they now had an oil burning fridge. Otherwise, even Nigel's appetite would not have been enough to deal with the turkey.

How could Kirui have got the news so soon? Did the legendary bush telegraph really operate? Were there systems of communication the authorities knew nothing about? Of course there are, Ellen admonished herself. In every country there are. Nigel did not really believe it. He could only picture resistance networks with radio transmitters. Kirui must be getting old now, but to think of his strategic marshalling of his equipment, his familiarity with their personal tastes, his ready smile, cheered her up immensely. She would give him a hundred shillings a month now (Jack need never know) and rejoice that he had a son going to high school. Angela was thrilled when she heard the news. Njoroge mildly approved.

120

Kirui arrived according to promise, slouching along the track in gaping boots two sizes too big, looser-jowled than he had been, his hair a grey stubble, his teeth more eroded. His greeting were joyful all round, enquiring after Bwana and Angela, showing a photograph of his* younger children, reassembling his kitchen tools, shaking his head over the state of the tea-cloths. Without being asked he produced his old magnificent mango crumble for dessert. The household seemed complete again.

Complete without Jack? The thought had seized her unawares. But one had to face it. Uncle was gone. Nigel and Angela were in transit, an extra blessing when their paths touched, but the childish intimacy had faded as they were forced away to boarding school, segregated by sex, colour and the complacency of the Kenya born. Perhaps it would have been different if she and Jack had ever actually set up house together, as mother and father had once done. It now seemed incredible that the Croydon drawing-room had ever existed without its Wilton carpet or the high-built suite in its chintz covers, renewed from time to time yet always looking the same. But here the setting was pre-arranged. She had edged her way into a routine already set and Jack's need of her receded with its familiarity: there had been no dramatic start, no dramatic ending. Uncle would not have impeded her but she had never known how to impose herself upon the house. The things that had been bought significantly new were the cot, the pram, the nursery curtains and then years later, as the young people became restive, concessions that showed up the consistent, acceptable shabbiness – brighter curtains, a proper dressing-table with a mirror for Angela's fourteenth birthday, and Nigel's guitar and a storage unit (do you call it?) for his airfix models.

It was when Angela was sixteen, thinking about going in for nursing, rebelling against school, chapel and the dominance of nuns, that the discoveries of Olduvai burst upon the world. Professor Leakey and his wife were able to demonstrate that man's earliest known ancestors had walked erect, made tools and windbreakers, and established themselves into permanence, right here in East Africa, by ancient lakes and retreating forests. Of course, there had been pointers to it. One ought to have been aware. But now one had to be proud of being an East African human of the most precious vintage. It tickled the fancy.

But it boggled the imagination. For when you tried to explain to students how important this was, shutters immediately rolled down. It was not only Adam and Eve who kept up a rapid fire of dissent: they had managed to subsist vaguely in the same dream-time as Chieng' and Mumbi, but they had grave objections to being equated with a lot of old bones in Tanganyika. What made it harder on the imagination was that the ground was swept from under your feet: the Rift Valley had not been there. The familiar lakes and plains were a divine crumpling of the original terrain: these man-creatures had actually lived through the tumult, corporately seen mountains thrown up and valleys eroded, skirted a dozen changes in the configuration of waters, obstinately given birth, evaded predators, snatched fire from the burning mountains, piled stones against the cooler air of new high places, hunted, eaten and survived.

Did one dare guess how many? Enough to find mates and reproduce themselves. Enough to leave weapons recognisable before they wasted away in generations of use. Enough to communicate to their young that learned experience which, alone save for a blessing, can ensure continu-

122

ance through all hazards. These days you could ring birds or spray paint on to elephants to record that they had been counted, but in those endless ages no intelligence but the Almighty's stood outside to keep count.

Such a pitiable handful of remains on which to build a world-shaking statement, and yet each of those uncounted people had died. Some bones, no doubt were calcined in forest fires or volcanic craters, others crunched up by man-eaters or submerged under young lakes, crushed by falling boulders or relentless hoes. But some of the dry bones lived.

Chapter 7

The phone shrilled and Martha moved reluctantly towards it. She was not at ease with strange voices. Mercifully it did not ring very often. The call was from the hospital.

"Is that Mrs. Smith?"

"Mrs. Smith is not able to take the call." She could speak to the nurses in Swahili with confidence. "May I take a message?"

"Mrs. Smith was to come for an eye check last Wednesday. Does she wish to make a new appointment?"

"Mrs. Smith is not able to go out without her doctor's permission. May I speak to Dr. Mrs. Kapila about it?"

"Dr. Kapila is not in at present. May I ask her to call you?"

"I should be grateful. She knows the situation."

Martha explained to Mrs. Smith: "It is about the eye test. We shall ask Dr. Kapila about it."

"What do you mean, Kapila?"

"Rozhan. Surely you remember Rozhan?"

"Yes, she went to do medicine. But she was a Shah."

"Kapila is her married name. She married outside the community."

"Rozhan – oh yes. She was in Lilian's class, wasn't she?"

"That's right, Lilian and Marion and Rozhan, all in one class. Eighteen years ago they joined form one."

"Is it so long? I remember the first day I met you, Martha. Kirui was a dear but he was getting so old and slow. I'd promised to keep him on till his son got through high school, and he was finishing that year and everything had been paid for. I said to Sister O'Brien that I wouldn't know how to get him home if he collapsed on us. Angela

was just leaving school, you remember, expecting everything bright and shining when her friends came to stay.

"Sister said to me, 'I've got the perfect help for you, Mrs. Smith, and a good thing you'll be doing for Kenyan woman-hood if you give her a helping hand.' You remember the way she used to talk. She sent you to see me in the staff-room, Martha, and I've been thankful for it ever since."

"So have I," answered Martha, "for I never could have got Lilian through on what I was earning at the hospital."

Nyambura – Lilian – had sailed through intermediate and was offered a high school place. Miracle of miracles – a girl. In Martha's time there had been only one high school for girls and even there they did not take the certificate. But how could she find the money? (Njogu will come, they warned her. When there is dowry to be paid, he will sniff it out and take the lot. Well, it was not for dowry that she was doing it. And there was no dowry, as it turned out, from that strange white man, but presents sometimes and the certainty that he would look after his children.)

Martha asked advice of one of the white sisters at the hospital, quite an old lady, unmarried and very strong.

"You sign the paper," Sister said fiercely. "We'll find a way. Don't let her miss it. Dear God, how I had to fight myself to get that paper signed: it's time for your girls to fight too. She must have the chance. Come and see me on Monday. But *sign the paper,* do you hear, or don't come into my sight again."

She signed it. Was she crazy? Two hundred shillings a term for four years. Uniform. School fund. Caution money. Reading slowly, she could make it out. Anyone would think she was mad. Local Native Council could be asked to help. But what was local? Who was the head of the household?

Could Sister O'Brien know what a risk she was taking? Incredibly, she did know.

"One of the teachers," she said, "needs help in the house. I've given you a splendid reference, Martha, so don't let me down, now. You will have to live out of town but the children can join you during the holidays. OK? You will have to squeeze something for people here to feed them duing term-time. They could walk out to you at weekends at a pinch.

"You must finish your month here in the laundry, but Mrs. Smith is able to wait. Her own children are almost grown up. This is the first intake of African girls to the school so I have arranged for you to pay for the first term in three instalments. It won't be easy, but you must do it. Then they will know that you are serious about Lilian's education and are doing your best, supposing there is any hold-up later on. Sister Patel is transferring to Eldoret, so her daughter's Nakuru uniforms won't be needed any longer. I've got them here for you, and you must alter them to fit so that Lilian doesn't feel uncomfortable with the other girls. And here is a couple of pounds from me towards the odds and ends . . .

"When you take the girl to school for her interview ask to see Mrs. Smith. She will explain to you about the work. I'll talk to the Hospital Administrator before you go to give in your notice."

Martha could hardly gulp a thank you.

"Go on with you. People were good to me too when I got the scholarship."

So the miracle happened; *kûgeria nì kuo kûhota*, the old people used to say, trying is only succeeding.

Since that bargain was made, she had managed somehow, always knowing there was a place where she was needed. Not that the money had been all that much to start with, but there was no rent to pay, a little garden of her own, an advance sometimes when it was necessary.

She did not have Lilian circumcised. For once she was ahead of things. The law now forbade it, and goodness knows what Lilian's husband, Jim, would have thought if she had given in. She had not thought the refusal was a strongly religious thing, when the old women came sniffing round the door and hinting before the school holidays began. She just felt the whole hugger mugger was unnecessary and unhealthy. A fatherless girl had to live in a new world and discover the rules as she went along. Perhaps Sister O'Brien, urging girls to high school, never realised the question had been raised.

Mrs. Smith certainly would not have realised it then. She stood at a more clinical distance than Sister O'Brien. Perhaps the nurse, poring over your specimens, pulling your pants down, tickling your ribs, was always more in the know than the teacher, standing aloft and pouring new knowledge down your throat. But Martha could see a virtue in standing at a distance. It left you room to make your own moves. Not like that Mrs. Grant who had seen everything and could not stop talking about it. Good things might come out of that, but something also was lost.

Since that first meeting, Mrs. Smith had spent fourteen more years teaching. By now she must know that her Kikuyu girls, however protected, were within the hypnotic range of the circumciser, and that the circumciser herself was not some antique skin-clad figure but possibly handled your money in the market or scrubbed floors in the Town Hall. But she would not link that knowledge with Martha or Lilian because she saw in them reflections of herself and Angela. Or did she? She had pressed Martha's hand during that cold church wedding of Lilian's in Nairobi: a few relations had, it is true, raised a traditional song or two, but there was none of that preliminary feasting of the two families, the pointed thumbs and the dancing that would embrace the *Mthungu* and bind him to the clan. Mrs. Smith had not even been at Angela's wedding or gone to take leave of her ageing parents. Perhaps she understood the feeling of being left out.

Martha admitted that she could not really comprehend Madam's life in those years that stretched before the preparations for *Uhuru*. She had never known the Bwana when he lived at home or Nigel and Angela when they were little. From her father she knew the routines of morning coffee and evening drinks, but she did not know families as he knew his to the most intimate detail – when to lay one place less, as though to suggest that the young master had already said he would be out late, when to serve the cheaper sherry, when discreetly to clean the car that was thought not to have been taken out. At least the family appreciated him and assured him the blessing of a natural death. Employers were always vulnerable to servants, she thought, disclosing intimate portions of their lives. But servants, if they had self-respect, could to some extent fend off the intrusions of their employers. Only when you were old and lonely you might betray yourself and not remember how ignorant of your real life these strangers were.

Next morning was wet and cold. The windows were shaded by the overhang of the roof, but rain slanted in on to the verandah and dimpled the puddles in the hollows of the pathway.

Mrs. Smith thought it proper to get up for breakfast most days, but this time Martha was intransigent, bringing a tray to the bedside table, propping up the pillows and tucking a shawl over the sleeveless nightgown, which still, secretly, scandalised her.

"Now you just stay there, Madam, till the fire is drawn," Martha commanded. "I can't have you getting a chill on my hands and the telephone cut off as likely as not with all this water about. I haven't even got across to open the hen-house yet, the rain is that heavy."

Mrs. Smith gave in. She had learned over the years that there are times you have to let servants have their own way. It is the same with school classes. You sometimes humour them, provided you have good general discipline. And some, like Lily, like Martha, were more friends than adversaries.

Martha's daughter, Lilian, had been among her first batch of African girls. There were some boys too, but it was the girls who stuck in her memory. Lilian and Marion were among the clever ones who had earned their place the hard way: some of the others were daughters of good families, a privileged minority who faced their exams with the advantage of know-how as well as know-what. They always had the crispest blouses in the class, the most shining hair, and had been schooled on how to behave in a mixed community. But as time went on there came more loners with frayed collars and wild eyes, some of them tongue-tied, some compulsive talkers. Some of them dropped out because the money could not be found or the cost of finding it themselves had proved too high. Their questions had to be answered. They would not accept the sidetracks down which you could lead the Indian girls, who sensed the need to circumvent some terrible indiscretion.

129

"Madam, we hear that Her Majesty the Queen had decided not to *produce* any more. Is that so?"

"Is it true that the British invented concentration
camps during the Boer War?"

"If half a crown is two and six pence, then why . . . "

She learned a lot during those two or three years when
independence, docketed for twenty years ahead, somehow
crept up and overwhelmed them. Physically the girls astounded her and whole sets of assumptions were shattered.
She was no longer amazed to find a woman married and
divorced buttoning herself primly into a school blouse to
start the climb from form one. (Some younger sister must
actually have provided the primary certificate.) Some girls
demanded fees from their fiances: others locked themselves
into servants' quarters after school to avoid attention,
reading frantically, living on bread or bananas and cold
milk. Some felt that with their school uniform, they had
already achieved their hearts' desire and need not pay
attention. All were admired, envied, manipulated, bargained over. Some had a range of ability that astounded
her. Others had to be led gently from revelation to revelation.

She learned to know them by their place of origin as
well as their names. Pronunciation often served to define
them, but some spoke more correctly than the boys, having
been so solemnly winnowed out. Mary Muthoni. Hellen
Aoko. Fatima Ali. Peris Shishia. Tabitha Mulwa.

She took them out as much as she could, to inter-racial
Girl Guide meetings, the Post Office, the Law Courts. With
literature you could always find a connection. The lady at
the bakery commended their good behaviour. "Though I
still say we should look after our own first."

Who are your own? The lady in the bakery was not on the best of terms with her in-laws. What was the content of "look after"?

Ellen was worried about Mrs. Banerjee. Over all the years they had not got on to first name terms. Mr. Banerjee had had a heart attack in his shop and died suddenly. "He worries about things," Mrs. Banerjee used to say. "He does not like anything to change. *He* doesn't wear a *dhoti* as his father did. Why should . . ." but she always broke off guiltily. Brothers and relations engulfed the family. The children, all working, seemed to retain their individuality but Mrs. Banerjee sat white-robed, diminished, as though stunned. You did not know whether they would accept flowers, whether to take your shoes off, what you could say, silenced by the polished floors and the scent of spices. What loss, what status, what choice . . .

Mrs. Banerjee kept on the flat above the shop, though a brother-in-law took over the business. A few weeks later, she was back in school, assertive in class, reserved in the staff-room. She no longer fasted on Thursdays. The flat, where Ellen occasionally called for a ritual cup of tea, lost its mystery, retained its bright shiny surfaces and occasionally smelt of cigarette smoke: but in school, of course, in mixed company, it would not do to admit the weakness. Leela, working in an accountant's office, played the record-player at high pitch and revolted against her mother's classical music, but there were always enough school-girls eager to learn the dances.

Every year they took part in the Nakuru Festival, which included a mixed race choir singing plaintive English songs and a sheep-shearing competition for African shepherds. Some of the farmers got huffy because their cattle wilted, refusing to drink the heavily chlorinated town

131

water. They ought to have foreseen that. But there were other things they ought to have foreseen. People enjoyed themselves. Mr. Holmes was photographed with Kimalel holding his trophy. Wilberforce played a cornet solo.

"These days I feel quite comfortable about helping with the clinic," a farmer's wife commented at the Club. "The *bibis* are trying so hard, some of them even teach one another to read. You see, in the long run they want to be like *us*."

Ellen doubted whether that was what they wanted. Nonetheless, even this thin concept marked a change. She just hoped the lady would express herself more graciously if one of the African officers .who had been given temporary membership of the Club should actually turn up. Ellen could remember that at first she would get the wives' and babies' names mixed up in the quarters, although there were not many of them. This lady came from a much bigger farm, but also she had had many years to get to know it.

One of the first demands the African students made was for a Christian Union. This caused consternation, as most of the teachers were Moslems or Hindus. There was a Mr. Fernandes, who taught art and technical drawing, but he was a Roman Catholic and so debarred, by some logic Ellen could not follow, from participating.

So she was asked to help. Staff patronage of societies was not always demanding. Some threw themselves into table tennis or girl guides: others put in a minimal presence at the debating club. She supposed she could spare one afternoon a week after school and bash out some hymns on the piano, remembering the patchy devotion of her own childhood, the resonance of "Onward Christian Soldiers", the bitter sweetness of "My Song is Love Unknown". The commandments had been impressed upon her early with a conservative modern interpretation – you do not go to the cinema on Sundays, you write to your parents at least once a week, you do not cheat on tax returns or spread gossip that you are not sure is true. But her use of prayer had been perfunctory: it had not occurred to her that she could be used by the prayer.

So it was a shock to be asked to give a testimony, and she put the students off, "Let me see how you want to organise things first". Then the hymns they wanted to sing were not from *Ancient and Modern* – "Have you been to Jesus for the cleansing power?" or "Shall we gather at the river", and she could not find the tunes. Altogether, it was a bit of a disaster, until Miss Shaw stepped in to fill the gap, and for a time clouded her relationship with certain students. Eventually they managed to get back to terms of mutual respect, discussing, "Tiger, tiger, burning bright" and Milton's sonnet on his blindness, in the bland terms of reasonable religion. After all, any Hindu could do that without getting into dangerous waters.

Miss Shaw was an American missionary with delicate oriental colouring. Ellen never dared ask whether she was of immigrant stock or had ancestry from what she had learned to call The Nations. Miss Shaw was unassertive and very well-groomed, careful not to give offence to any non-Christian, eager to bring the girls through to Christ as well as preparing them for exams. Through what? Ellen wanted to ask, but saved the question for a more private occasion. Some of the students saw Bible knowledge as a practicable alternative to Urdu or Gujerati: they were not bothered by mugging up something they didn't *believe*. After all, you didn't *believe* that a solid table was composed of a fretwork of atomic particles or that cold had no physical existence like heat, but that did not prevent you from meeting the requirements of the General Science paper. Even if you were a Luo speaker and found the Bible less challenging than French, there was no particular difficulty in alleging that a man loved his wife as Jesus loved his bride, the church. Both formulae were pretty remote from everyday experience.

Miss Shaw, who did the round of a number of schools and youth clubs, changed her schedule once again and said that she was sorry Mrs. Smith had been troubled. It was too much to ask of anyone who had not yet made a Personal Decision. When she came to that point, the Lord would instruct her as to the priorities. She handed over a little booklet with a list of bible references.

Ellen dutifully looked up the references and found that every text was familiar, though she had not been in the habit of daily reading since she left school. It seemed a bit much to talk about girding on the whole armour of God – one was not a priest, after all – but to hold fast to the truth and be faithful in marriage and be prepared to meet a few fiery darts, that went without saying if one had had a Christian upbringing. She had had the children christened, of course, and taught them "Now I lay me down to sleep" and "Thank you for the world so sweet". School had taken over the rest.

She took Miss Shaw out to lunch, rather than seem to sow dissenion before unbelievers, and pointed out that she was able, with a good conscience, to proclaim English Composition to the thirds and French Grammar to the first formers without making a Personal Decision about it. She offered subjects according to her inclinations and training and accepted new methods so far as they commended themselves. She appeared to get on all right in terms of student response and examination results.

134

Miss Shaw fiddled with her fork and for a time avoided Ellen's eye. Then she swallowed defiantly and launched into speech.

"I know you care for the girls a great deal, Mrs. Smith. That is why I hoped you had already, in your quiet way, taken a further step. If you do not see the need for it, I would like you to pray about it.

"You people feel so safe. These students, especially the girls, know they are walking on a minefield, and it takes a dose of what you perhaps call old-time religion to get them through it. It is better to know when you are in danger than not to know.

"You see," she glanced around cautiously, "myself I spent my childhood in Singapore, part of it in a prison camp. I know you wonder how I come to be here, and I ask myself if you can understand what such an experience means. My mother died there. It was beyond her strength, of course to do all . . . all that was required of her. My father – it was an act of charity in him to be so sure he was my father – brought me out in the end. He was an American business man. He had nothing left, of course, but I was able to make up the school time I had missed, and that is enough to praise the Lord for. They do not . . ." her eyes were still wary, "the mission board do not like me to talk about it. They would wish the students to be protected from these things. So do not repeat it, please. But if I show you how much the Lord can save one from, I think you are able to bear it." They joined hands. Then one of the schoolgirls came in with her mother, and they turned the conversation to other things.

A few years later, when Nigel was getting married to Ann and Ellen went up to Rumuruti to discuss the arrangements with Merle and Ralph, she raised the question again.

135

Merle had been an Australian missionary and was the sort
of person you could talk to, not starchy but willing to help
out at the Catholic dispensary or settle a dispute among the
labourers' wives, whatever came to hand. "It's no good
working up emotion," she had said. "Read your bible, go to
your church, whether it's very inspiring or not, give yourself
enough quiet time to take directions from God." But
somehow the time was never very quiet, the services
seemed irrelevant, the bible came in mostly for poetry
lessons. There was nothing decisive about that.

The one thing to be noticed about these fervent Christ-
ians was that nothing seemed to surprise them. Merle could
talk matter-of-factly about drinking black milk from gourds
flavoured with charcoal, walking away from a confrontation
with cattle rustlers, accompanying patients with running
sores to the STD clinic. When people lived humbly with
miracles and voices no fantasy of science, no extreme of
degradation, was beyond their contemplation. Ellen hoped
she was not incapable of learning something new, but she
was always being surprised.

Martha's first coming to the household, a landmark
linked with Lilian's presence in the classroom, was over-
shadowed at the time. Ellen had just lost her father, Angela
was leaving school, and the pace of public change increased
from day to day. Those African violets on the window sill —
she never looked at them without remembering her daughter's unexplained contempt for them as a symbol of everything outmoded. (Well, in her young years even the name of
an aspidistra had become a joke.) Yet she had never removed them — tough, self-propagating, thriving on half-light,
they made a kind of sense to her.

Angela liked Martha, but had infant memories of Kirui.
Still Martha was quicker, neater, spoke Swahili well and

136

understood English. Some awful thing had happened to her husband, so that Mother said it was better not to ask. Their prefects had had tea-parties with the seniors from African Girls High School. It was not very easy, but they had learned things that upset them. Georgie, whose own father had been killed in Italy before she was born, had been in floods of tears.

Angela was restless, waiting for her exam results, bored at home and preoccupied with clothes, since so much of her recent life had been spent in uniform and the old holiday outfits now looked juvenile to her. There were no white girls of her age nearby and those who were younger would soon be going back to school. Mrs. Banerjee invited her to Leela's birthday party, but there was some constraint. R. J. Patel put on an end of term supper for the teachers and their families, but Angela brooded in a corner: had she not sacrificed goodness knows how many years of her life to the company of teachers? The Mistri girl, on vacation from Vellore Medical College, dazzled the other young people. The Patel daughters, shop-wise, fluttered around her. Long earrings, they thought, would suit her. (Earrings for goodness sake! She was hardly out of school yet.) Mr. Fernandes begged her to consider going on to sixth form. *Sixth* form? What for? The sisters did not seem all that eager to retain her. Even her mother, lips pursed over the report, did not think it worth persuasion. Mother – look at her, crunching up the *jelabi* – wearing the plain amber chiffon dress she had made when the Queen Mother came, heavens, *three* years ago at least, disastrous! (It all showed on her face).

"Your mother is so marvellous," Miss Shaw whispered to her, "always the same, never seems to get any older!"

Mutton dressed up as lamb. You could say that again. And lamb dressed up as lamb, you trotted beside her.

Auntie Mavis, she remembered, was more with it, though a bit on the heavy side. Even Gran. She supposed her mother must be missing Gran and Grandpa, but she never let it show. All buttoned up.

Jack came for Christmas, sensed the atmosphere and whizzed Angela off to Nakuru. They came back with a candy-striped button-through dress, a set of costume jewellery and high-heeled shoes.

The buttons will gap as she grows, Ellen thought, and the white part will stain. And how can she step out of the house in those shoes? What does Jack know about the way girls live? I remember being furious with my mother too, but one could never, never let it show, only lock the little girl flowered frock away in the wardrobe and make an excuse to wear the old one.

There were jewellery for Ellen too, Celtic style, in a little box on Christmas morning. What Jack did do, he did well. Nigel arrived, now looking almost comfortable in a suit and tie, bringing an umbrella for his mother and a fluffy sweater for Angela that sent her into ecstasies. Perhaps, after all, they understood one another. Nigel and his father got some obscure satisfaction out of an afternoon spent together at a spare parts dealer's.

Ellen and Jack discussed Angela in the old bedroom to which he returned without any strangeness or excitement. Perhaps she could take a secretarial course before the nursing interview came up: it never did any harm to be able to bash a typewriter. Of course, she would prefer Nairobi, anyone would. Her friend Betty had been sent off to study in England and her mother was taking in paying guests, to help with the expense. Perhaps that would do for three or four months.

138

It did. Angela was overjoyed and at once began to write adult, matey letters. Betty's mother showed her how to make over the school blouses into exotic, low-necked patterns that she could wear to classes with a tight black skirt. Betty's mother explained some of the difficulties between generations. Betty's mother had actually been accepted at London University herself, but joined the army instead and got married, so she never went back. Betty's brother had gone to South Africa for university because it was cheaper and he sounded like a terrific guy. The other paying guest was a research student from America and she was so much into an affair with an African politician that you hardly saw her really, but Betty's mother said you had to live and let live. (With the rates they were charging, Ellen thought, you couldn't bypass any American, especially if she was eating out all the time.) Nigel occasionally took Angela to the pictures on a Sunday, but there did not seem to be any foursomes.

At Easter, Ellen took Angela to Kampala for a spree on the little money Father left. Uganda was secretive, prosperous, and soft spoken. Stepping off the train, they marvelled at the luxury of Kampala, the shoe stores, the fabrics. There were no white farmers in Uganda, yet the crops prospered and the college was making a name for itself. That was as far as they got. Tanganyika remained a wild place in their imagination, where Greeks settled and Ernest Hemingway roamed at large. All the same, Nigel had his part of the treat there, climbing Kilimanjaro from Marangu as was fashionable.

In due course, Angela was accepted at the European Hospital, pinned her hair up, took on an hour-glass shape divided by a tight white belt (egg-timer you had to explain to her, since she attached no meaning to hour-glass, had no

139

inkling of Edwardian fashion-plates). She mastered her sensibilities as to pus and vomit and became a different girl altogether. On leaves accumulated after night duty, she appeared laden with textbooks and muttered about urethra and sulphonamides. She might no longer have scorned a date with Basker Banerjee, but Basker had been fixed up with a B. Comm. from India: her father put up two *lakhs* for the wedding. Angela talked earnestly about the Nightingale spirit with Martha's Lilian, who had come for half term, and Sister O'Brien took her out to lunch and expanded on deprivation as a factor in illness. You did not get to see many deprived patients at the European Hospital or Princess Elizabeth, but Angela opened her eyes wide and understood that some had shut themselves too long away from treat- ment, a few had grown up undernourished in wartime camps or hideouts. She examined babies in the staff quar- ters and privately wondered how she could get to see a cir- cumcised female patient. After all, there were not enough European Hospitals to absorb all the trainees.

The logs crackled on the hearth but for a long time the chill in the air remained. Martha lit the kitchen range as well, to reinforce the heat, and made a batch of scones and roast potatoes to justify it. But the air, even indoors, remained overcast.

Pathetic fallacy, Ellen remembered, suiting the weather to the incident. Why not suiting the incident to the weather? Wordsworth skating on a brilliant frosty day. Only a fool would want to skate when it was wet and muggy. Little ships making for Dunkirk through brilliant sunshine. In fog there would have been even more casualties at sea, though perhaps fewer on shore – one less in particular. But "they shall not grow old as we who are left grow old": could one really picture Stanley as a bald-headed

140

dentist of 58, perhaps married to a bossy nursing sister, father of systems analysts and telecasters? It did not bear thinking of, to change the past. If they had not done their courting through a dry, dusty summer, would Nigel and Ann really have opted for Australia? He might have become a pale-faced teller in a High Street bank in Tunbridge Wells or Macclesfield, while Ann battled with immigrant classes and the boys boasted of their ancestry in multi-racial Kenya.

Suppose, if there had not been a summer thunderstorm, she and Ken, that spindly King's student she had met at a college dance, had gone on the river as they had planned instead of to an unintelligible play in a little theatre that left them nothing to talk about . . . Every choice narrowed down the future choices posed to you, and yet the moral choice was always the same.

"The trivial round, the common task

Will furnish all we ought to ask . . ."

What common tasks remained? Well, she must write to Angela. If her hands were still too stiff, she would dictate the letter to Mrs. Mistri next time she came. She must check in the book for Nigel's boys' birthdays. Marion also had written to her. It was through Marion that she had encountered Mr. Mwangi again at Speech Day.

Parents' day 1962 went according to pattern. The displays of work were tidy, the refreshments were enough to go round, the girls shyly presented mothers, fathers, uncles (in some cases you took a second suspicious look at uncles, especially if they were on the young side), the teachers were resplendent, the dances went without a hitch. Ellen did not for a moment recognise the proud father who was battling towards her through the crowd.

"Mrs. Smith! Didn't I tell you Marion would be in your
school? Well, here she is in form three, and it's the first
time I've been able to attend. I have been, as you might say,
unavoidably detained."

"Marion? Of course I know her. But I didn't realise she
was yours, Mr. – Mwangi."

The name came back to her with an effort from the
child's report sheet. "You mean you are the same Mr.
Mwangi who used to eat the dictionary in Mr. Galsworthy's
office?"

"The very same, plus a few bumps and scratches, Mrs.
Smith. And how is the lieutenant?"

"The – oh, you mean my husband? He's pretty well, Mr.
Mwangi, working in Kitale now. He got a few scratches
himself after an argument with a tractor and we thought
perhaps farm life doesn't agree with him."

"No Emergency trouble?"

"None to speak of. A couple of cows – the odd stores –
what you expect in time of war, but none of us were hurt,
thank God."

"Time of war. Well, yes, you could call it that."

"And yourself? Marion's mother?"

"Oh, she's fine, Mrs. Smith, but not here today because
someone had to stay in the shop, you understand. As for
myself, well, you said I'd swallowed the dictionary. Maybe
that is what made me hard core. *Persona non grata* is
another way of putting it."

"A very different way of putting it, I would have
thought. You had a bad time, then? Mr. Galsworthy never
forgave them for taking you away from him."

"Well, it would be dull inside, I suppose, if you had no
claim to distinction . . . I called in at the insurance office, of

142

course. He has a Swahili fellow doing pretty well there, and I definitely prefer being self-employed. So you might say we are all happy."

"But how did you manage to bring up your business so quickly? I mean how long . . ."

"The tough ones need the longest treatment, Mrs. Smith. You must be aware of that. But you may remember a little talk we had about keeping your lines of retreat open. My good wife and some friends had everything under control. Were you never a girl guide, Mrs. Smith? Be prepared is the motto we got from the Baden-Powells, isn't it?"

"I was taught it, yes. But perhaps the thing you are prepared for is not quite the thing that happens."

"That's because you have too much trust, Mrs. Smith. Perhaps your good husband did not train you as thoroughly as he did us. 'Know your enemy' is what he used to say. Hard cores always do that."

"I'm sorry. But Marion is doing well at school. Perhaps she won't have quite as many problems as you had."

"You help her to meet them, that's all. And remind her I'm not a bad prophet. Before you were two years old, Marion, I told your teacher you'd get admission here and see, you have."

Lilian came shyly up with Martha.

"Here's another pair of my girls, Mr. Mwangi."

"Yes, I know. A good pal of Marion's, the young one is. There's not all that much I don't know, Mrs. Smith, that happens round here. And my regards to that military man of yours."

Increasingly that proved itself to be true. Mwangi had an interest in providing sacks to Jack's employers. He set up new stores as the land was divided. He soon became a councillor.

There was a new girl in Ellen's third form English set, Una Patil – a tall, quiet young person with bobbed hair and an excellent command of English. She had been transferred from a school in Mombasa and was living with an aunt and uncle whose son had been in Ellen's primary class.

"Mrs. Smith," she whispered. "I should like you to meet my father."

"How nice," she replied automatically. "I know your aunt and uncle but I don't think I have met your father."

"I am sure not, Mrs. Smith," replied a cultured voice, an England-returned voice, she immediately decided, and rebuked herself for the classification. "I live in Mombasa, you see, where I am an advocate. I miss Una a lot, but the older children are studying overseas and we thought it better for her to have a change after her mother died last year. The climate here is healthier, too. And we have excellent reports of the school."

"It is a pleasure to have her here. I am sorry, I did not know about her mother."

"These things are not easy to speak of, Mrs. Smith. I could not have wished my wife to suffer longer, but one can be very lonely without people who care for the same things. That is why I am happy that Una responds to literature. It gives us something to share."

"Ah, yes. I see that she comes from a reading home. I am glad that you have that interest in common. It is a pity to be bowled over by a book and have no one at hand to share it with."

He was slim, ageless, with liquid Parsee eyes. It was absurd to suspect that he glanced at her left hand before

144

pouncing on the teacup she was holding and getting it refilled.

"You may feel a bit isolated here?"

She felt herself flush.

"My husband is not much of a reading man and he works at a distance. I am fortunate to have the school to keep me busy."

"Indeed yes. And it must be a joy to be bringing students together in the classroom. Not, as we so often do, separating people over some trivial issue in court."

The headmistress called her to deal with some other parent's query, and she excused herself, knees trembling. How absurd! Five minutes conversation and a film-star smile. At her age, how could she give way to emotion like a teenager. Besides the communities – devil take the communities! How much of Europe had she, brought with her, callow as she had been for all her reading, to be coarsened and abraded by Jack's beer and skittles? That was not fair, she knew. He had learned his trade and pursued it; even if he had no real affection for the land and stock, he nurtured them.

Poor Jack. He never pretended to be more than he was, and the children were content with that.

"Goodbye, Mrs. Shah, it has been so nice."

"Goodbye, Mr. Sheikh. Yes, some handwriting practice in the holidays will make all the difference."

"Goodbye, Mrs. de Souza. Jacqueline is making wonderful progress on the piano, I hear."

"Ah, Mr. Patel, how is Rajendra doing in India? He was one of my very best students in the primary school."

"Virginia, greet your mother for me. I know you are disappointed that she couldn't come, but she has to stay home till the baby is a bit bigger."

"Mr. Gulamali, that was a beautiful trophy . . ."

There was a letter from Jack in the post.

Dear Ellen,

Hope this finds you well as I am at present except the leg plays up if I am on it too long. Nigel says he is doing all right at the bank. Can you give Thomas three hundred towards the feed? I will see you right when I come at the end of the month. I said I would send it but they could not give me an advance at the bank. Paddy and Dick send their regards and hope to see you next school holiday. But I will be down before that without fail.

Your loving husband,

Jack.

She cried herself to sleep.

Later that year Jack got pleurisy: Paddy phoned to tell Ellen about it. She was not to worry: they had a daily nurse in to him, more comfortable than moving him a long way to a suitable ward. (Suitable means white.) Jack did not want her to wonder why he was not coming down at the end of the month. Easter holidays would start next week: why didn't she come up for a day or two? No need to rush.

So she did not get there in time to speak with him. Two days after the first call they got a nurse (cowards!) to ring and say it was all over.

She had him buried at Kitale. It was where his friends were, and it was not as though they had been attending church anywhere. Angela, summoned from hospital, burst into tears at the graveside, certain her nursing could have saved him. But she had never seen much of him since she

went away to school. Her routine was not touched in anyway. Nigel, looking so young in a formal suit, stood embarrassed and silent. Ann Besser left her parents' side to stand
beside him. Nigel had spoken of visiting their farm when
he spent a few days – more often than was strictly necessary – with his father. Ellen looked at him with a lift of
hope.

There was no addition to that old will made when
Angela was born, nor was there much to leave, but the lawyer sorted all that out. Ellen was only glad to sell the
remaining fields, now at last unencumbered, and keep just
the house and yard. Some of the farm men belonged to the
cooperative that wanted to buy the land: she wished she
had known; they might have fixed it before, if the law allowed. And for all her painful detachment, she would take
pleasure in the continuity.

"Don't you think you'll find it too noisy, mum? Lonely?
You could get a flat in the town," Nigel said, "For yourself, I
mean. Angela and I are sure to be moving on. You could be
a bit comfortable."

Comfortable? When did she remember being comfortable, or hanker after it? She was not lonely with Martha.
She could teach a few years yet. (There would be something
to invest, but not enough to live on). "You're safe when you
have a house of your own," Mother always used to say.
(Mother who had never handled a bank document bigger
than a birthday cheque). What sense could she attach to
"being safe"? And yet the house was there with its familiar
instruments of living – the blue and white china, the heavy
dresser, the wood range . . .

It was no good moaning about being a widow – she had
been a widow for years. Perhaps Jack had been a widower
too, with no one to look after him. It had been his own

147

intiative and it never occurred to her that he might mind. She left Nigel to sort out the few things Jack had had with him at Kitale – he had bought a radiogram from some white farmer in a hurry to leave, and a whole row of Reader's Digest condensed books. Perhaps time had hung heavier on his hands than they had thought. From the farm-house he had faded away almost as much as Uncle.

By the time the term started Ellen was back in a safe routine: the other teachers had made their polite condolences, but their real concern for her showed in continuity. Everybody was very kind. Una's father sent a card in impeccable taste. Mr. and Mrs. Mwangi came round with a couple of chickens and seemed surprised that the house was not full of people. Beatrice sent a melancholy letter, Mavis a cheque for fifteen pounds and reminder that they had a spare room any time. The schoolgirls, according to their nature and upbringing, hugged her, offered flowers, pasted up cards or demanded to know why she was not wearing a black dress or a white sari, shaving her hair or discarding her earrings. Lily, hearing the news from some remote connection, telephoned impulsively from London. Martha ordered bread and sugar when necessary and produced trays of tea without being told.

The dismemberment of the farm went on in the daytime and she could close her mind to it. A grader was at work on the road. Mr. Mwangi was buying the farm manager's house and setting it up as a grocery store. There did not have to be many goodbyes. Mr. Thomas, in any case, was going to get work as a surveyor, having completed his studies and somehow found time to get engaged to be married.

"Survey," Jack had remarked one day when he came down for his usual conflab with young Thomas, "that would have suited me well if I had ever had the chance." In all their young years he had never referred to it.

Ellen was one of the longest-serving teachers and liable to be roped in for painful interviews.

"Theresa, you seem to be getting rather fat. Do you think you should get advice from a doctor?"

"I wonder if you have quite understood what the P.E. teacher was telling you about sanitary protection?"

"Mary, your mother tells me she gave you money for the Girl Guide weekend camp but Miss Shaw did not see you there."

Little by little, you got a glimpse of their life outside the school. Was someone else cross-questioning your own children, delving into areas you dare not explore, taking for a granted a different code from that you had taught them?

Angela – it was easy to see the signs – had an eye on an super young doctor in pediatrics, and had secretly hoped he would offer to come to Kitale with her when Dad died, but someone tipped her off that he was engaged to a secretary in Mombasa. She rolled her heartbreaks into one and observed Nigel, who had paid many visits to Kitale (though it took all day on the OTC bus) and seemed to be very thick with that teacher, Ann Besser. Well, Nigel was twenty-two now and seemed quite at home in his window at the bank with rolls of notes and his special keys. He had a little flat and a motor scooter. Ann was his own height, slender and light-haired. She dressed indecisively, print frocks and cotton skirts with blouses. They said the youngest children loved her: she was never put off by bleeding knees or snotty noses. She wanted a multi-racial class, but the fees were such that only three or four Africans managed to make it. Nigel did not seem to mind, but what would happen to the children, Angela wondered, after this *Uhuru* that even when I was at school seemed a distinct dream, but now it is just round the corner? We shall be swamped or go away.

She put the question to her mother when she went up for a long weekend: everything seemed the same as usual, mother busy with school work, Martha quiet and efficient, the men around the farm coming up to her to say sorry and looking as though they meant it.

Mother explained that Njoroge was one of the group buying the fields. That would suit her ideally, and the price seemed fair. Se had had long discussions with the lawyer.

Leave? Leave to go where? If they had thought of going away (she used the plural notionally) it would have been when the children were still at school and could have looked for free training in UK. Now that the grandparents were dead – you could see where the guilt still rankled that she had not organised herself to go and see them – where would she go? Do you look for a new teaching job at fifty? Or land on your sisters?

Ellen was certain where she belonged. She also knew that her successful pupils would be so much in demand that they would not come down to superseding her, as might happen in England, offsetting the safety net of social services. Of course for the younger ones it was different. In twenty years' time the Lilians and the Marions might be shouldering them out. (But not, she told herself, if they had London degrees. Had she failed them in that?) Those holding land were already running scared. Mr. Galsworthy was planning to join his family in England. He had an apartment in Nakuru now, for the Holmeses had sold the dairy and were already gone. Paddy was quite confident about his feed business. (She did not say that Paddy had

150

made clumsy overtures to her soon – far too soon – after Jack died. She liked old Paddy but he was Jack over again. No widening of horizons there.)

Even old Mrs. Grant was preparing to leave, in her own good time, once she had got her old retainers settled, but that was because she was over seventy and had no family at hand. You couldn't see Lady Eleanor Cole turning her back on things, could you now? Or Lady Farrar? The Happy Valley crowd had dispersed, but the backbone of the old families still remained.

Angela was uncompromising. She wanted to go to England when she was qualified. (Don't we all want to go somewhere, thought Ellen, but once upon a time North London had seemed enough.) She didn't mind nursing black babies but being bossed around by a black doctor was another thing entirely. It was all very well for Ann with her missionary connections . . . The name hung in the air. Mother never asked "What Ann?" Well, it would do. But could Nigel really . . . ?

"I suppose there is always work for nurses," said Mother, unsurprised. "Provided they respect whatever doctors they get. You would have to get a job here, save for a bit. We shall have to see how the farm sale turns out. There is a hundred pounds for you from Gran. Perhaps I did not tell you about that. I kept it for something important, you see." (A hundred pounds was the price of a rat-proof grain store, prefabricated. She had needed to keep the secret.) It was a good thing Father sent it for each of you when she died. Because although he was the business-like one, he left very little."

They found that after lavishing every comfort on Mother in her last days, he had commuted his investments into an annuity. It must have been either that or sell the house, and he would not have wanted to share his retirement with Mavis's aquarium or Colin's evocation of the Raj. In any case, the house was damp at the foundations and needed roof repairs. It did not fetch much. Mavis's second son was having to get married in a hurry, so the family were glad to let him have the pick of the furniture as a corporate present. There was a will, of course, all ship shape, but after the fixed legacies – £100 to the cleaning lady, another £100 to the British Legion – and the expenses , there wasn't much to share out. They sent Ellen the Dutch reproduction pictures and a cheque for £165. She hoarded it for a while, then spent a lot on those holidays. Father had always urged them to see more of the world than he had himself.

Angela went back to Nairobi reassured. Black people were planning their future, becoming permanent secretaries and army officers, flying off to America in droves for education. Brown people were telling you how much better India was but not noticeably going there. (Well, there would be no room.) She had her plan too, unless, of course, somebody really dishy were to turn up before she left. The England she remembered at six years old was strange and stuffy but, according to the newspapers, swinging London was going places. You did not get housemaids, of course, but there must always be orderlies to do the rough work in the wards, and delicatessen if you did not feel like cooking for yourself in your flat. They surely wouldn't expect you to live in a nurses' home, not in London. (Her mind did not dwell on provincial towns, let alone the countryside. She had had enough of *that*, for goodness sake.)

Look at that old pupil of Mother's she was always raving about, Lily something. There had even been a magazine article about her and she was always on English TV, Auntie

Beatrice said. Mother made a face about that – how uppity Bea and Colin had always been, and could not see that Lily was *vulgar*. She could have been a serious actress, but instead she always had to hog the limelight with her own shrill points of view. And divorced. But then she had done pretty well out of it, and always travelling.

From England you could afford continental holidays if you got a good job, and her tutors took the professional journals that were the gateway to good jobs. You could even give Lily a ring: "I am your old teacher's daughter." "But how lovely! Could we do an interview on nursing in Africa? How to keep your looks in hot climates? Freedom and friendship? Could you meet me at a little place in Chelsea?" Angela hummed as she arranged the flowers round an unconscious patient.

Nigel also hummed as he cashed up and banded the notes, though he had been referred in some of his exam papers and so might not be thought to have anything to sing about. He had dated a few girls in Nairobi, without going steady, but Ann was different. Really this was not a bad job for getting to know a lot of up and coming people across the colour-line, and that was important to Ann. Of course, lower class workers did not use the bank, but then you came across them anyway.

There were big celebrations for independence – Madaraka and then again Jamhuri – entertainments in the school, processions in the town, feasts on the farm, services in the churches, parades, a new flag, a new anthem. So many holidays: Ellen could not object when Nigel asked if she would mind his spending Christmas with the Bessers, sharing a lift, and of course, he came back engaged to Ann.

She did not brood upon it: there was so much else to do. She was able now, to sponsor the Mistris' application to the club, a small return for their kindness. The Maendeleo ya Wanawake asked her to join a committee organising literacy classes for women.

Virginia, a rather shy student, had invited her to lunch on the occasion of her confirmation, in a cramped house overflowing with crocheted chairbacks and small children: she had been delighted to go, but she had become vulnerable to Mothers' Union and Ladies' Guilds. Pronunciation of bible names in English was one thing: flower arranging, she had to protest, was beyond her range.

Ann came down for Easter to get better acquainted and proved to be a sensible girl. She had done her teacher training in Australia and her younger brothers had decided to settle there. She and Nigel thought of doing the same. Ellen raised her eyebrows. It was not that she minded, but reading had led her to expect an unnatural air in that desiccated continent, an unbiblical fauna, a foreign grammar. Nigel up for the weekend was forced to be frank.

"We have branches there, you see. The Bank might be able to fit me in. They hate to let people go once they have spent time on them. But honestly, mum, it is not as though I had a proper training. Jobs like mine will all be africanised in the next couple of years. That stands to reason. Already there are cashiers with better exam results than I have and good English too. If they keep any whites, they'll want graduates or accountants. And some of the present fellows would be in the Royal College now if they'd been a few years younger." He tried to keep reproach out of his voice.

"You could maybe join us when we've got a bit settled. Ann's people too. Depends on how it goes. Don't forget that little bit of bother at Lanet." (The mutiny came to nothing, but some people panicked because the road was closed.)

154

"I don't intend to go anywhere. But you're young yet. Think about it."

"Well, we can't afford to get married right away. But Angela is in a hurry to leave. Perhaps we could have the wedding early next year, make it a family affair before she goes."

"That's up to you. And there's a hundred pounds from your grannie in the bank for you. I don't know whether I have ever told you."

One day during the holidays, Una and her father came to call. They had not telephoned in advance and Ellen was wearing an overall, cleaning out the cupboards in her room.

"Why, how lovely to see you," she exclaimed, meaning it, and calling Martha to attention in the kitchen. "You have not gone back to Mombasa yet, Una?"

"No, not yet, Mrs. Smith. My father had to make some calls here first. And we hoped you wouldn't mind."

"I am delighted, my dear, that you both could come. Do have some tea. My daughter Angela is around, on leave from the hospital where she is training, but some friends have taken her out riding. My son also works in Nairobi."

There was a weighty pause.

"You must be missing your husband, Mrs. Smith?"

"Well, as I think you know, he had been working away for some time. I was not used to having him close to me. I suppose I am quite self-sufficient."

"You do not think a close family is important?"

"My parents were inseparable. I therefore assumed that to be the normal case, but perhaps it is not. If you move into a different life-style, it cannot always absorb all of you."

"I suppose not. Have you formed a theory about it, Mrs. Smith, a set of principles?"

"A theory? Well no. Probably we were taught – rightly or wrongly – *not* to abstract. Would you say there is a theory about it in your community, Mr. Patil?"

"It seems to be thought that women should be encouraged to advance themselves so as to give adequate support to their husbands' interests. I don't know whether it had been theorised beyond that point."

"And have they been adequate?"

"In my own case so much more than adequate that perhaps the theory does not go far enough. It would be interesting to see how it works out where there is less identity of purpose."

At this point Angela came bouncing in.

"Mum, mum – oh, sorry. I didn't know you had visitors. How do you do? How do you do? Greta's dad is going back to Nairobi. He could give me a lift if I can be ready in half an hour. You wouldn't mind? It would save me waiting for the minibus tomorrow . . . You will excuse me, Mr . . ."

"Of course, dear. Go and pack. I don't suppose he'll really be back here in half an hour. Una, do have a look at these magazines. You may like to borrow some . . ."

"You know for yourself how demanding families are, Mr. Patil. Even if they are not here all the time they dominate one."

"And is that not enough to compensate for the loss . . .?"

"They are what remain of what was lost, isn't that so?"

"They are, but they will not always . . ."

"Can I take your blue holdall, mum?"

"Of course, of course, but don't let it get sticky . . ."

"You do not ever come to Mombasa in the holidays, Mrs. Smith?" Una enquired. "With Angela, perhaps."

"Not for many years now. The heat is a bit too much for me." (That was a silly thing to say.) "Will you go back there when you have finished form four?"

"I suppose so. But my father will be leaving for India soon."

"Oh dear! You mean you are leaving for good?" She did not attempt to hide her consternation.

"Perhaps not for good. But the family exerts certain pressures. I have not found a way to avoid ..."

"Well, I think that's everything. Mum – excuse me, won't you – Greta will come to pick up the boots and she can take the records from my room ... Una, what will you do when you leave school? I say, is there some more tea? Do you see how much dirt you've got on that overall?"

"We had better be moving out so that your friends can park. Thank you, it had been so pleasant ... Next year, perhaps?"

"Oh mum, thank goodness," cried Angela afterwards. "What would Greta's dad have said? You know how anti – he is."

Ellen was glad when she was gone and she could finish off the cupboard. It was ridiculous, at her age, to keep imagining things.

Chapter 8

The cap of a red biro lay under the hedge, enmeshed with cobwebs and fallen leaves. Surely it must have been discarded by some schoolchildren along the lane. It could not have lain about for four years since she did her last marking. Yet it was in the odd corners, in and out, that paraphernalia collected – a bent drawing-pin, a rusty bull-dog clip (such as girls bought in pastel colours and stuck in their hair nowadays), a beaded net cover you used to put over the milk-jug or jam-pot. Angela found them intolerable. She would rather let the flies drown, like big black commas floating about in a story that was not properly constructed.

The last years of teaching had flowed by without much to distract Ellen from the joys of discovery and the anxieties of exam results. Nigel's wedding in Kitale had not really been a landmark: that two-piece she had bought in Nairobi was the same one that Martha, thirteen years later, hopefully regarded as "best". Ann had made a conventionally pretty white bride backed up by little girls of every colour. Merle was a bit embarrassed about serving drinks, but Australians were supposed to toast the Queen at weddings and, when local dignitaries turned up, felt bound to toast the President as well.

Angela had gone to England later the same year and Nigel and Ann left for Australia in 1966, eager for a new home in which to start a family. Ellen envied them the long journey by sea, now unfashionable, but her imagination could not share it. Perhaps four degrees south was meant to be her limit.

She had been careful. She told herself she would go to England for Angela's wedding. She pictured Mavis bulging out of trouser suits, doing aerobics, feeding her pet fish.

Beatrice would be growing old gracefully, still mourning the death of empire. The school would be comprehensive but surely more orderly than the one she had seen in the Sidney Poitier film. The Cathedral precincts could hardly have changed all that much, as the new rich moved into period cottages and the rural workers were glad enough to swap them for council flats with all mod. cons. You could go by motor-coach to the continent or even stop over from the aeroplane. The boat – if it was still running – would take too long.

But when Angela finally decided on Tim – the turnover of doctors had been quite rapid – they were very casual about it and timed it for the exam term, so she did not go. Angela wore a sort of draped two-piece in a fearful yellow, while Tim's mother, all horsy teeth and silk jersey, looked more impressive over her shoulder. Ellen wondered whether the drapes concealed the reason for all the hurry and thought, in any case, she would postpone the visit till the birth of a grandchild, but no grandchild ever arrived and Tim and Angela had come to see her instead. He was tall and very English with something like her father's voice. They had dashed in and out of the house, in between visits to game parks and medical seminars, set for a stopover in Greece on the way back. Angela had long flowing hair, that time, no make-up and a seemingly endless stores of tracksuits. They fired off questions about cholera and sleeping-sickness. It was term time. They left her exhausted and still curious. Nothing was said about her going to visit them. Angela seemed to grow by stages like a butterfly. Perhaps next time it would be all layered hair and little black dresses. But in a butterfly the showy stage was the last one. Her mind closed to it.

Ellen's expensive two-piece came out again for Lilian's wedding. You could not see through Martha, whether she was pleased, shocked at a white son-in-law, grieved at their going away. It seemed only decent to make an occasion of it and, next year, to drive Martha down to the airport in style to see them off to England. The two matrons (as Ellen's mother would have put it) shared a room at the church guest-house, doing their duty by their family.

There had been, in the meantime, that bit of bother in Kisumu. Things were going a bit offside in Uganda. But here in Nakuru everything fell into place, as more and more African children filled the school. The Asian families still greeted her in the shops and garages, but more of the younger people were going away – driving buses in Manchester, changing travellers' cheques at kiosks in London, manufacturing calculators in Canada, introducing Mughal cooking to Aberdeen. She was jealous for her best students: some of them got into university locally or did private courses in accounting. She hated to let them go to places where their skills were commonplace. The overseas schoolarships were mostly for African pupils or potential pupils, and one longed for more time to prepare them for cold weather, reticence and the unfamiliar shape of regional speech. They would not have the years of running-in to a society that were the alternative to asking the right questions. But she had survived and so would most of them.

New neighbours fitted quickly into old slots. The lady from the old Holmes' dairy had a daughter in the school, and would sometimes call in to borrow a cookery book or ask advice about gadgets which Ellen was not herself acquainted with. Her English was getting more fluent all the time, and she always welcomed you with tea and home-baked scones. The husband was a bit more abrupt,

160

especially if he found you driving slowly along the rutted road when he wanted to get past, but they got along. Young girls from the settlement would appear at the door, sometimes, offering to sell eggs or enquiring for work, actually eager to peer behind the curtains and marvel at the rows of books, the plates arranged on the old dresser. Martha would shoo them away, but if Ellen were home she might ask them their names and encourage them to practise their primary school English. Against that small acquaintance her own students emerged with a new clarity.

You had come to take them for granted, no longer fragile or faultless, though still vulnerable. For those who dropped out, poverty-striken, pregnant or overwhelmingly nubile, there would be others, just as able, who had been excluded by some accident but would make their way in the world at less expense to their families. Mrs. Maini, taking over from Mrs. Desai as Deputy Head, was as severe on hot combs and chemical straighteners as Miss Church had ever been in the thirties on permanent waves. Multiple plaits were an abomination to her, nail varnish a recurrent assault of the devil, but she never seemed to mind how much vaseline the girls used. If they had none, they clogged the pores with smears of toilet soap.

Such rules became harder to enforce as more African ladies joined the staff. The older ones felt a need to reinforce their authority with carefully set hair and expensive skirt suits. Those who followed, with science teaching diplomas or American degrees, ran to floppy clothes and even, occasionally, lipstick in the daytime. The students did not seem to mind. They saw their own emancipation as only a matter of time.

Ellen got used to it, though there was a constant hazard of failing to recognise people. One might, she thought, devise a shadow play around these changing silhouettes, but suppressed the thought and progressed dutifully from *Elizabeth Refuses* to *The Government Inspector* and *The Trials of Brother Jero*. She might not have managed to restrain herself if she had not retired before the basket-handled craze in hair-dos reached its height. The great-uncles, when she was a child, would make great play of peeling an orange into an intricate lattice-work, the fruit and pith rolling untouched within it. After the second time, you had to grit your teeth and pretend not to be bored: uncles were entitled to respect. The picture came back to her every time she saw the stiffened coils of hair, raised like horns and waited (hopefully) for one of them to be caught on a cupboard handle or impaled on a curtain ring. Well, the other ladies did not refrain from comment on her repeated purchase of the same, comfortable sandals or the gradual acceptable greying of her hair, for which they constantly off-ered remedies. She felt she could call it quits.

And for the Music Festival, as confidence grew and the apparent age of teachers decreased, dabs of chalk, increas-ing exposure of the flesh, rhythms of more than one dance tradition, transformed the well-groomed choir of the set piece into a troop of maenads. One had to be pleased with the artistry, the illusion, especially when it came to exploring another Kenyan culture than their own. But it was a far cry from those early classes, more absorbent than assertive, and it was by no means easy to reassure the parents. They had expected that their daughters would emulate the European, that they should imitate the Maasai was, as they put it, "Something else again". She would have loved to get Lily's comment on it.

In 1971, with cries of treason in the air (it sounded like Tudor history: Ellen was teaching *A Man for All Seasons* to

162

form four) she went to Mombasa for Una's wedding. It was marvellous to be near the ocean, though the smell was insipid compared to northern seas, and people seemed to be trying – unsuccessfully – to reduce it to the stature of a tourist attraction.

Una had read literature in India and worked on magazines. She was marrying a South Indian Christian in the protestant Cathedral. Parsee men were in short supply and nobody seemed to mind. Her stepmother was elegant and assured, young enough to have children of nursery age, but not too young. Everthing was beautifully arranged and Ellen, blinking back the few tears the ceremony always excuses, exchanged news with half a dozen old girls and discovered that she had taught a cousin of the bridegroom when he was a mischievous schoolboy in standard four.

She was glad to stay a day or two in the guest-house, exploring Fort Jesus and the old town, and to join a tourist party up to Gedi and Malindi. After all these years, it seemed as exotic as Alexandria or Paris. Perhaps she would come again when she retired, even take a trip to Lamu or Lake Turkana. Or overseas. But you keep busy and all of a sudden you are sixty three and no longer working.

It was not long after Ellen's retirement that Lily Beach wrote to propose a visit. This was a delight, only slightly tempered by the reflection that repairs to the house and furniture, postponed over the years, could not reasonably be undertaken on a pension. She wrote the next day.

Dear Lily,

What a lovely suprise to hear that you may come and see me! We don't actually feel that we live in the back of beyond – everywhere is dead centre for somebody – and I hope having a home in Kenya to refer back to will help your perspective on women's rights.

163

You will find me shabby but more or less unbowed, a widow, as I think you know, with a son in Australia and a daughter in England. I have only been there once since 1938 when you may remember the marvellous send-off party the school gave for me. By that time I was already sure you would carve out your own niche in society more confidently than I have ever done. Between your occasional letters and those of other old girls I have filled in with snippets of the English papers my sisters sometimes send. Beatrice, the ex-India one, dines out on the fact that I once taught you – or perhaps goes out to tea would be a better expression, since the old professional classes hardly "dine" any more, and the new ones, which you represent, do not seem to make a conventional division of the twenty-four hours.

We do not have a TV set here and I don't suppose you would find our local programmes very exciting. I don't think, from what I know of you, that you will be put off by our rather old-fashioned living standards. However we shall both be sensible enough to tell the truth if you need to be nearer to town or I show my age under the impact of the fashionable world. Probably most Kenyan women are preoccupied with bread, not butter, without a thought of jam. Girls' education had forged ahead, but there isn't much time to speculate on sexual equality, let alone fantasy.

Phone me from Nairobi so that I can arrange to meet you in my old jalopy or lead you in if you have a hired car. If you can't get through to my number (above), leave a message with the dairy (7797) who are very helpful when we are cut off.

With all best wishes for your safari.

Yours sincerely,

Ellen Smith.

Putting the letter ready to post, Ellen sat down to consider her position. It was only when the doctor chivvied her about the varicose veins that they remembered her age and pushed her into retirement. Not that she was not getting tired – forty years since she began teaching, and only about four she had stayed home because of the children. Only a matter of months she could say she had ever given to Jack. Poor Jack! Thirteen years since he died and five before that he had lived in a boarding-house. Not that they did not have, in prosaic terms, relations, but in terms of imagination they scarcely met. For all that he was not a dull dog like her. At least she supposed not. Does anyone really know? What does Lily know about her cast-offs? Does she think them inferior creatures, sacrificed to her career? God help me, she thought, I never wanted a career but the children had to eat.

She had never bothered her head about taking citizenship. She had not paid her stamps in England either, in fact, did not well understand the system. In any case, she could not face the cold and the strangeness of everything. She could not half make out Angela's letters – TV dinners, hypermarkets, polystyrene, motorways, Chinese takeaways, breakfast nooks, dining alcoves, sandwich courses, duvets, ponchos, video cassettes.

So now it appeared she would have to pay for a residence permit every year to stay in her own house. She did not understand all that but the lawyer would see to it. Well, she would not use so much petrol now or so many decent clothes, or lunches and teas out, though a meal in town does cheer you up. She would not like to sacrifice the telephone just yet, or the car: sooner or later she would be considered too old to drive it. After all, it would not fetch much, being third-hand, after nearly ten years. Martha's pay was little enough, though more than the law demanded, and the scale of "keep" had been altogether transformed. Well, if you wanted companionship, you must have something to share.

She used to see the farm as nothing but a drain, but now there was interest on the money, fortunately, for the pension was not going to cover the cash transfers to the children at Christmas and grandsons' birthdays, and the little things for her sisters and the old farm hands when they came round. For now that it was settlement land, long acquaintance established her place among decent, hard-working neighbours who would bring vegetables for sale, cheerfully give a shove when the car was stuck in the mud or request her signature to petitions to have the road improved or a new school put up.

Suddenly she was weary. Why had she not retired at sixty, even fifty-five? She could still give private coaching or enlarge on the chickens or make jam for sale as white women did in the old days. Would she feel better if she had a holiday? Could she afford one? Holidays had always been few and far between. She had spent a few weekends with Merle at Rumuruti. She was glad now that, before Jack's accident, they had once taken the children to Tsavo to see the animals, like tourists. Sometimes she had to take school parties to the music festival, and when Angela and Nigel were training in Nairobi you could go down to a hotel for shopping and to the dentist's and meet them without too much invasion of privacy. Now people she used to know had left the country or were dying off. Surely she could treat herself to a couple of nights at the Devon Hotel after Lily's visit.

Would Lily make sense of this? Beatrice and Mavis would understand it, though they might not get around to

166

saying so: both had been tethered to a society now swept under the mat. Well, they had a world that was kind to the old (not that she thought of herself as old yet). Free doctors, automatic pensions and special bus fares when you showed your card. It was hard to imagine it. And all revolved round the telly.

Beatrice acknowledged change by goggling at the box and delighted to tell her friends that her sister had actually taught Lily Beach how to speak properly: she so much admired a girl who could break away from her background like that. Now Ellen had just fallen in love with Kenya, and teachers had so much to offer in developing countries. My dear, she would not hear a word against the new order of things: how marvellous to stay on even if there were no jobs for your children! Of course India was quite different, so many specialists prepared for independence that there was absolutely no need . . .

Lily's mother would have understood it in her time, only incredulous that there could be resources beyond the pension. Occasional letters from Lily and printed interviews had supplemented her distant memory to give her a very clear picture of Mrs. Beach.

A couple of marriages – no kids – were not really landmarks for Lily, but Annie Beach never got over it. "For all we see you on the box, Kath is the one who made her bed and laid on it," Mum said. The fifties saw Lily already on TV and by the sixties she was being remarked on in *Private Eye*. She got a brief spell in Parliament and was always talking about sexism, which to Mum's ears sounded dirty. "Perhaps it's as well your father's passed on. He liked a woman to keep her place. One of the biggest crosses he had to bear was seeing me go out to work when he couldn't."

Still, Lily had a nice big flat in Golder's Green and seemed to keep herself going.

"You've got to stop thinking about how much a week, Mum," she used to say, coming on a TV commercial now and again, and then a play about the bomb in some draughty little theatre without proper pretty dresses or anything, and speaking to women's meetings here and there and conferences and even Oxford University (and her divorced twice!) and writing letters and letters and letters. Yes, she explained, there were funds to cover the stamps and the typewriter ribbons and the air fares to America or Germany.

She wrote to that nice Miss Mountford who had been good to her in grammar school and now gone to live in Kenya, and she wrote back about how black and brown girls had to struggle for their education. Well, struggle, you could say that again. Mum still did not feel quite at ease with Lily, going on using her maiden name as though she had a right to it, and suspected that one day Lily might be taking her off on the box. But she had gone with her on one of those speech-making trips to Bonn, just to be able to say she had been in an aeroplane and seen foreign parts. (Lily never seemed to find her way to Majorca or the Costa Brava.) And, Germans and all, they had treated her right, though the food was a bit on the heavy side.

Lily missed her mother when she died in 1972. But she did not miss the things her mother missed – armistice night on the wireless and Lyons Corner-houses, Ivor Novello and Caruso, trams and changing into your summer clothes at Whitsun. Lily lived for the future and felt desperately sorry for those willowy schoolgirls engaged to some stuffy Patel or Khan without a by-you-leave. (That an eager Patel might be tied to an avaricious fourth-former, that an idealistic Khan

168

might look anxiously for signs of philanthropy behind the rings and bangles did not occur to her.) She agonised for bright girls pinned down by strings of babies. The pride of motherhood, the family praise, the tumble and caress of small things at play had missed her. She felt complete.

Mrs. Smith, mother of two, grandmother of two, widow of one, teacher of thousands, felt by no means complete. She had no illusion that a post-marital romance or a more glamorous career would have completed her. Nor did she have any inkling that surrendering her life to God might have done so.

It was a rainy day in May when she jolted into Nakuru to meet Lily at the Stag's Head. She was very conscious of the spattered mud and the faulty windscreen wipers. She dressed as for school, chiding herself for being nervous but remembering the twenty-six years that stood between her and the shabby post-war London that was now considered glamorous. Where had the years all gone? The first half into rearing the children and letting them go: the second? Well, there had been other children – Meena and Lakshmi, Lilian, Marion, Wilkister, Sara . . . After all, there was something to show for it.

Predictably, Lily was already the centre of a crowd in the lounge, but she sprang to her feet to embrace Mrs. Smith and include her in the group.

"I'm sure you all know my old teacher. She must have taught some of your families too. Honestly, Mrs. Smith, I should have known you anywhere – that's what comes of having a good bone structure – the beauty lasts." (Lasts my foot! Good bone structure – does any husband notice that?) "Mr. Fernandes says he's actually seen me on the box during his travels, and Matthew recognised me from a picture in the paper, but I told them, if I hadn't had the luck to get

169

into that school and be taught by you, I might still be selling cabbage like my mum and the height of my ambition as a girl was to get my photograph taken at the local *palais* – dance-hall that is, in the days before the disco."

"And I bet you did that as well," put in a smiling, rounded man with a porkpie hat and a scar on the left hand. She ought to know him – Kamau? Waweru? No, of course it was Councillor Mwangi, who had started the grocery store on the settlement but now sub-let it. She had to fumble for the name and Lily had got to know these people already. Mwangi had put on a lot of weight since his daughter, Marion, was in her school. The younger ones, of course, went to Kenya High or Limuru.

"I did too, when we came back on holiday after being evacuated. Winning foxtrot with Jimmy London who got his lot on the beach at D-Day. Of course, you had left by then Miss – Miss Mountford, as we all thought of you. I was dead scared the head would see it in the paper.

"'My girls never wear lipstick, and they know better than to attend dance halls or cheap films!'" (The mimicry was perfect: Ellen could see at once Miss Church in her pawky flesh, angular, kindly, and earnest in her illusions. "But you see, Mary, in the *long* run it doesn't cost any more to have a spare pair of shoes and give them an airing: both pairs last longer." 'June, we cannot put *up* with this messy work. You must go to bed if you are tired in the evening and get up really *early* in the morning when you are *fresh*.' Oh yes? Rolling over Meg and Ruby to get out of the bed, not able to go to the sitting-room because Tom and his mate are sleeping there, no place to sit in the scullery even if you dare put the light on, because it's always dark on account of the height of the Buildings, for all that it's better (they keep drumming into you) than Ma and Pa ever had before, when they were young, thanks to Councillor sodding Peabody.

"But of course it was a local rag," Lily added, "and the Head wouldn't have been coming up from the country for the holidays."

"The girls must have envied you all the same" Ellen wondered if she would have noticed the item herself, if she had been there, and what she would have done about it. "Would that be a brother of Violet London's? I just remembered her when you mentioned the name."

"That's right. Violet was older than me, so she went into the ATS and got married to a Canadian. I don't know where she is now."

"Well, this talk of long ago won't interest you gentlemen, but it shows you we remember our old students. How is Marion getting on, Councillor Mwangi?"

"Fine, Mrs. Smith, just fine. She has two little boys and works in a bank. Only that man of hers is getting involved in politics, and I always say politics is a good way to make money but a good way to lose it as well.

"But I think you don't know my son? Matthew, Mrs. Smith is a good neighbour of ours and we were all sorry when her husband Jack Smith passed away. We served together in the war." (Jack Smith? *Jack* Smith?) "Matthew read law at Dar es Salaam and is finishing off now at the Kenya School of Law. You'll be seeing him around."

"How very nice. Yes."

"Well, time to be buzzing back to the office," said Mr. Fernandes, including a silent colleague in his gesture.

"Oh, but excuse me for a moment. Are you a connection of my colleague Mr. Fernandes who used to teach . . . ?"

"He was my uncle, ma'am. Intellectual part of the family, they tell me. Died before I finished at the Duke of . . . Jamhuri, myself, I suppose you knew that."

"Yes, I heard and was sorry."

The Mwangis also got up to go and Lily insisted on paying for lunch so that she could be, as she put it, a bit clued up before facing Mrs. Smith's household.

"The household is Martha and me so that is no problem. After Jack died I sold what was left of the farm to a cooperative. Some of our old staff belonged to it and are still neighbours, so you can cross-question them about the bad old days if you like. I kept the house, which is mercifully near the road. Well, we call it a road. So we manage very well. I haven't had time to get bored with retirement yet."

"So Martha is the maid or what?"

"Martha is maid and companion and housekeeper rolled into one. She came to us – seventeen years ago, when the children were already leaving school and the man who used to help me was due to retire. She was a widow whose daughter had qualified for high school, which was something marvellous in those days. And so it has worked out. Our children have gone away and we continue in our set ways. Martha can have both rooms of the staff quarters and she can use my bathroom and kitchen now that we are on our own. She would be a good person for you to interview."

"Will you interpret for me, then?"

"Oh, there is no need. She only went to standard four, but teachers were strict in those days and she lived in a place where English was commonly heard. If you don't hurry her, she will be able to speak with you more confidently than many of our form one girls today. But between ourselves we use our own kind of home language, a bit of this and a bit of that."

They drove home under dramatic skies, through the gentle landscape too much like England to arouse Lily after the spectacular crossing of the escarpment by minibus that morning. There was a lot to digest before you came to precise interviews. For now she tucked her feet up on the old couch and drowsed in front of the wood front.

You did not see fires like this in England any more. Not unless you went to one of those classy country clubs where someone else had to tidy up the mess. She was thankful Mum had been spared that, the last years when the rheumatism was so bad in her hands; she didn't have to come down to a cold room in the morning and brush out the powdery ashes and rebuild the fire, shovelling coal from the outhouse into the scuttle on the hearth. And yet Mum complained that underfloor heating was never the same. (It was not meant to be.) Even when she remembered the fire-bombs and the smoky glare in the sky, it was not the fear that she recalled. Perhaps in Kenya there was no need for fear of fire.

Lily had always been shrewd, whatever exotic guises she had had to adopt to make her public image stick. She would not be easily taken in, Ellen thought, arranging which schoolgirls she should interview in a clubroom borrowed for the purpose away from the still inhibiting atmosphere of the high school. She was glad enough to keep out of it. She had never had that bubbling energy, that knack of presentation, excluding doubt and pedantry, that made news, and yet somehow she had fostered it in others. She would have docketed her exhibits by tribe, community, sect, parentage: all her hints seemed swept away and a composite picture was in the making. Whether it was a true pic- ture or not she was perhaps too old any more to tell.

Sara, hair swept high with combs, uniform off centre to display a casual elegance, was hogging the scene.

"None of them cares," she cried dramatically.

Lily Beach was transfixed. Excellent stage material, good legs, a bit on the heavy side but all the tricks, her head was saying. Where can she get her training? Her heart was pierced by the eternal feminine degradation of it all. Her experience was asking the reason for this display. The resilient spirit she tried not to believe in was saying, "Thank you God for bringing me through: I have had my troubles, but we were more humane than this."

"You see, my sister-in-law brought the fees, but they say it is fifty shillings short. They nearly sent me home, but one of my teachers reminded them that it would cost me more than fifty shillings to go home and ask, and who would I ask, anyway?"

"Who gave your sister-in-law the money?"

"My brother, of course. He says he gave it all to her, but he doesn't say he gave her the bus-fare. She must have taken out the bus-fare, though she says she didn't. She has never liked me."

"Does she have money of her own? Where would she get the bus-fare from?"

"She has what money he gives her for food. And she trades a little when she gets a sack of stuff from home. It is up to her to manage."

"Does he give her enough?"

"What is enough? She is fussy. Gives the children fresh oranges. Who can afford that in a town? Besides, she ought to be able to get credit."

"Are not oranges plentiful?"

"Well, they cost plenty. And they are not like *food*, after all."

"And how long has your brother paid fees for you?"

"Since my father retired. That was five years ago, when I was in standard six."

"Your father has a pension?"

"I suppose so. But it is not like working, of course. And then there are the little ones . . ."

"Younger than you? How many of them?"

"Six, I think; there was another one due this term. They wouldn't think to tell me."

"But, Sara, that is a lot of money they pay for you, and then bus-fares and uniform and so on. Myself I was grateful that my people did not push me out to work as soon as they could. *Keeping* a great teen-age girl was thought to be burdensome in those days, let alone paying out extras for her. They must care about you . . ."

"But I am a bit of their property, don't you see that? They like being able to say 'We have a son in form six and a daughter in form three and another in form one.' They are sure I shall be able to get a job and pay it all back. And then of course they will get dowry for me when I marry. Probably ask for it in cash, too, like my sister-in-law's people did, and spend it quick so that if you want to split up you can't because there's nothing to pay back with. Oh, they know what they're about."

"But the other girls – do they find it just as hard? Are there none who feel happy and relaxed with their families?"

"Well, a few get new biro pens and soap whenever they ask. They don't know what it's like, having to scrounge a refill from a friend or rub your socks on a stone to try to get them clean. And making your pads last . . ."

"But surely you are better off than your mothers were? I was too." (For all the scraping and the frayed blouses: who would have put my ma in for a scholarship? And people giving you little talks about sponging down every day and keeping a spare pair of shoes.)

But Sara was carried away, saw herself as having an inalienable right to classes, maintenance, coloured back combs and success cards. The other girls stood around waiting their turn, consuming bottles of soda and thinking of the effect these intérviews would have when they visited the home places. Lily would build an agony out of it for British viewers but she would not be taken in by hysterics. Ellen, loving them, probing them, still shy of their secrets, wondered how they themselves would get over it.

She had no such fears for Martha, a person who could protect her boundaries as firmly as Mother ever had. Their adult lives, and their children's, had come together at a fixed point, but Ellen had never tried to probe back into what lay between the knife and the fire. There had been intrusion enough in those times without inspecting the wound unless one were invited to.

Lily was asking about education, and she was gentle in exploring the area beyond. Supposing Martha had stayed on at school? She might have been a teacher, but within the same confines of marriage, Emergency, dispossession. And if Stephen returned? A man must live his life. She had done what was necessary for the other two. There were no demands she needed now to make of him, except for his affection and his explanation.

Mercifully William had not needed high school fees; after intermediate he had been offered a place in a teacher
176

training college where you got pocket money. She had supplemented it – bus fares, exam fees – but that could be managed and he had a good job now, though not good enough for that lady wife of his. Only when it came to the wedding, he had had to find his own dowry – she had never asked whether Lilian and Jim helped with it – but cups, plates, sugar they had wanted from her, those fat Kiambu women with husbands and fields of their own, and it was accomplished.

When Lilian started training – great God, in the same hospital Angela had trained in, but Angela had finished by then – there had been the watch, books, some stationery; but then nurses always work for their keep. The rest was easy. Jim paid no dowry but she had the assurance that Lilian and the children were safe with him. The law, he had explained to her, would defend them in England even if he, unthinkably, did not. Lilian bought her a big hat and a costume for the wedding in Nairobi. Mrs. Smith had driven down with her and again, the next year, driven her to the airport to see them off. This had been hard, the child being not yet born, but they said there was no more work for Europeans in laboratories. She found that hard to believe, but of course he had the right to take Lilian to his own place. *Gùtirì wìtaga ithe wa ùngì baba*, they used to say, meaning, "There is no one who calls someone else's father dad". They wrote regularly and sent cards and now and then telephoned on special occasions.

At the airport, Jim had given her some money in an envelope – not to buy a wife but to say thank you, he had told her – and with this and her savings she had started to buy a little house in Nakuru. She kept thinking that one day she would go and put the house to rights – most of the rent for it had gone towards paying off – and set up some improvements in her old rural farm. But somehow the few weeks leave had never been enough.

"Did you feel that wasn't fair?" asked Lily, trying to avoid all the words that had changed their sense since she and Martha had been to primary school. "Did you feel you had missed out on *Uhuru*?"

"No," said Martha. "You can't have everything. I think we have had a fair share."

But she did not have the words to explain further. Njogu had died because of the fighting, even if not in it. They had expected a new heaven and a new earth, but in fact most people went on doing the same job in the same place, treading perhaps more firmly. Those who had dragged their feet or toadied before were those who could not face the new society. Father, discreet and obedient as he was, exploited in the vocabulary of these young been-to men, had never stood in awe of his employers. He had kept his bargain: she had tried to do the same.

Lily questioned and provoked thought, recorded, photographed, departed in a haze of affection and excitement. She was memorable but she had always been a disturber. Nothing settled down quite the same again.

"You said little Rozhan was coming to see me?" asked Mrs. Smith, calling Martha out of her reverie.

"Yes. You remember she came to see you after she qualified at Makerere? And now she is at the War Memorial Hospital."

"Yes, yes. She did very well. I think she was the first of my girls to graduate. She will see that I can walk again soon, before Angela comes. Your Lilian did very well too. Where is she now? I seem to keep forgetting."

178

"She is in England with her husband Jim. You remember coming with me to the wedding? They have three children."

"Yes, of course, of course. You showed me their picture. I thought Angela might go and see them. Will they be coming on a visit?"

"Lilian thought about it after Janet was born, but then she had Ian, and you know it is expensive travelling with children."

Expensive – you can say that again. Nigel came from Australia with the two boys once, a bit after Ann's father died, that was, and they persuaded Merle to go back with them. "Not again till they're off my hands," he said. "Break the ruddy bank, that would." And yet he came again not long ago, Jack – no, Nigel, I mean, getting red-faced and tousle-haired like Jack, but on his own. The children must still be at school, so why did he come? I can't remember. He sold the car, the same old Volkswagen that Jack bought cheap in Eldoret in 1957 because some of the Boer settlers were running scared already at the thought of African cabinet ministers. Nigel drove it down for me to use for school and Jack kept the station-wagon in Kitale. I must have been hard up to let Nigel sell it. Or was it the same one? No, I got rid of that in 1966 and took over Ann's when they went to Australia. They needed a decent price for it.

"Why did Nigel sell the car?" she muttered.

Martha was looking at her anxiously.

"You couldn't drive it any more. That was the time your arms got stiff, you remember? And it helped to pay the medical bills."

She shivered, remembering how Mrs. Smith had looked that time, her left side paralysed, her mouth twisted, and no one had yet had practice in interpreting what she said, her face a terrible pink, like those coiled ear-beads, or the mush of stewed rhubarb Europeans liked to eat (throwing away the leaves, boiling the naked woody stalks with sugar). Nigel had been sent for: they thought the end was coming. But the doctors had worked: it was nearly three years now. Some kind of control had been recovered, a new regime set up. A kind of inertia had settled on Martha herself, because all her active movement was now in support of that other life. She had some provision for the future, but her present was mapped out by necessity.

"Nigel should have listened to me," Mrs. Smith insisted. "He seemed always to be coming and going with lawyers and doctors. Spoke about selling the place up and taking me to Australia with him or sending me to Angela in England like a post parcel. This is my home. What makes them think they can push me out of it? Australia might make you think of Kenya in the early days: perhaps that is because when I was young we used to call Australians colonials, but now that is all gone and people get so het up over words.

"I get mixed up now, or perhaps everywhere is becoming the same, the shops changing to self-service and you have to leave your bag at the door and nobody knows the sizes any longer. I couldn't make out what Lily was talking about half the time."

Chapter 9

The fire was burning low in the big, stone-faced fireplace in the sitting-room. Mrs. Smith was slumped in the big chair to the right of it – Uncle's old chair – peering at the white, powdery wood ashes.

She was too tired to move, had rejected quite angrily Martha's attempts to guide her along to the bedroom or get her back in the wheel-chair. "Let me be, let me be," she muttered. "Cannot I have a say in my own house after all these years? You go to bed and put the rug over me. I like the fire."

So Martha, obedient though she looked worried, tucked the rug round her employer and made up the fire again. She did not go to bed as instructed but leaned back in the chair across the hearth. She had brought in some pea-pods in an enamel basin but shucked very few of them. The supper dishes were still in the sink: they had soup and sandwiches but she had herself offered the soup in a spoon and fragmented the sandwiches. Her eyes smarted with the humiliation of it. Long before, she had bolted the front gate and the house doors. She had not bothered to put the news on.

A fire was a comfort on cold nights, but it left the place smothered in dust next morning. Well, never mind. She would pay one of the young men on the settlement to bring her another binful of logs and kindling. Even when she was a young wife at home, firewood had become scarce and no one any longer carried the huge bundles her mother and grannies had bent their backs to. The fire – any fire – took her mind back to those Emergency days when you stood in the new village after curfew trying to make out which of the old homesteads it was you could see burning. When you went back to hoe your fields, the blackened shell of the house might still be standing but you did not expect to find anything left that you had not managed to carry away the first time. The family hearth and the evenings of story-telling lay far away beyond that. In Nakuru she had learned to use charcoal daily, and it burned the shillings away into white dust, sometimes getting finished when the maize was still hard or before Stephen had come in to drink the tea she kept hot for him. Stephen had always been a wanderer, and now might be wandering over the sea, feeding the engines of a ship, perhaps, polishing the brasswork or mending the tangle of ropes and wires. Her grandfather had once worked on the railway, cutting and cutting the piles of logs consumed by the engine, but now you no longer see open fire in the cabin; people have come to fear it. Njogu once took Stephen and Lilian to see all up and down the train while she stayed at home with baby William. But all these things lay back before the fighting and the fires.

Ellen felt a drowsy warmth as though a great weight had been lifted from her. She did not want to be disturbed. The fire glowed like – rubies, was it? All those precious stones somewhere in the bible, and, yes, there was a brooch with a red stone Jack had bought her once, red in the grate and the white stuff Kirui used to polish the pans with.

Coal fires had a more orange flame. In her childhood every living-room in a proper house centred on the fire-place, so you got roasted on one side and frozen on the other, sitting at a small table to do your homework, the cinders were dark and hard and the fender – polished brass in Mother's world but darker and less obtrusive by the time Mavis got married – was to mark off the bounds of safety. In all areas of life then there had been proper boundaries – private hedges, separate playgrounds for boys and girls, first class carriages and waiting-rooms, signboards inviting you to inspect maids', ladies' and matrons' clothes, areas of hygiene it was indelicate to know about till you were married, jokes that might be told at an ebullient family party but never on the BBC. Now the boundaries were all blurred, fences down, open-plan homes and offices you saw in magazines, men in the washroom of the YWCA, everybody called by a first name . . . Your classes in school all mixed, black, brown, hardly any white any more . . . And you no longer saw black as a colour but as a whole range of tones and textures – almost yellow, peach-tinted, supple brown, shiny boot-polished black, grey with fatigue or layered like old leather, coppery, opaque, pimpled or papery. You no longer saw even the rigid local distinctions of the old days – ears no longer looped, teeth not drawn or filed (but artificially replaced if need be), young women well-fed, well-oiled, fore- heads not furrowed by the *ciondo*, necks not straightened by the weight of the water pot, hairstyles of every natural and sculptured complexity – it was easy to mistake their place of origin. Indian girls in jeans with short tops, Mos-- lems newly swathed and occasionally veiled (God's gift to the plain girl), white girls with bare dirty feet and beads in their hair.

White one had always known not to be white, but no firm dividing line remained any longer between white and brown, brown and black. The almost purple tones of South India recalled the pale blue handsome Krishna of religious films, but also the bursting veins of the militant white drinker. Pale Aryan skins coming down from Alexander would look almost Nordic to the Mediterranean stock of crisped hair and salt-tanned hide. The weight of differentiation was too heavy. Her head was bursting with it.

Martha tried to straighten her in the chair, but again she resisted, drawn towards the fire.

Mavis's husband, Roy, had been cremated in a fire like that, just like an Indian. Well, the name fitted: Roy, with his lank, black hair and prominent features – nothing wrong with that for she herself could have been attracted by black, oily hair, but one was never free – that was a boundary too.

Mavis and Roy, Rita and Douglas had crossed a boundary when they moved to Southsea. It was not their sort of place, not really vulgar but a mistake of timing. The British public would soon find out that they never had it so good and set off in droves for the south of France and sunny Spain. Angela was puzzled by the place when she visited it. "Like going back to your childhood, mum," she wrote, unaware of the shudder she caused. In 1968, the two couples had moved the best lampshades and the aquarium into their family flats and let the rooms to students or temporary workers. There were no more full meals or family entertainments. They played bridge on Thursdays and enjoyed concert party songs taped from old-fashioned 78 gramophone records.

Tourists coming in from the continent only wanted to see the sights of London and old world villages . . . Even the Thames was dammed now, all she remembered of it far away before the barrier of fire bombs and doodle bugs. She had seen some of the results, the ash and dead spaces that followed the fire, but never been back to see a living Britain . . . Phoenix . . . never been back.

In the morning, Martha drew the curtains, long cotton curtains of grey and crimson with an occasional peacock flash of blue. They had been there ever since she knew the house: she did not realise what a defiant investment of personality that had been after the Bwana moved to Kitale and when Angela had complained of the drabness of everything.

184

Even then the complaints might not have succeeded if it had not been for the distressing business of Muoki. Kirui had actively approved the new curtains and been grateful for the old ones to cut up into bedding and seat covers.

An early, almost horizontal light dulled the remains of the fire. Ellen lay still, breathing heavily, her face yellow and waxy, perhaps a little more twisted than before. She clamped her mouth firmly shut against tea and refused to lie down properly, stiffening her head against the chair, working the rug between her fingers, closing in on herself against disturbance.

She was protecting Nigel inside herself, conscious of the safety of the firelit room, bare but better than she had expected, the anxious excitement of Uncle, eager to see a child about the place, the virtuous pleasure of having taught little boys who, after all, turned out to be not foreign but lively and familiar. She was also conscious of Jack's support, absent as he was and hardly missed from her sufficient preoccupation, but still a father-figure, engendering, nestbuilding, now protecting his household in thorny symbolic encampments out there on the edge. She huddled against the encroachment of Stanley's pain and her parents' far to the north, exposed on the beach-head while her baby must be cradled, mosquito-netted against harm. Again the boun- daries had failed her – the gallant claims of the BEF over- thrown, the line of entrenchments useless, the island home on longer invincible, only the one promise remained unassailable beneath her heart.

And now this skinny old Kikuyu woman – she recognised her somewhere from long ago but the name escaped her – was trying to prise her mouth open so as to force down the castor oil mixed with orange juice and the pains would start while your bowels racked you on the wide bowl

. . . They would make you lie on your back with your knees up and, fair enough, you had been expecting the pain, but the indignity, the public exposure . . .

Click, click, click. The woman was telephoning now for the doctor, and he would come and pry deep into you and, if what he found was interesting, call a student . . .

"Mrs. Banerjee, Mrs. Banerjee – hallo, yes, good morning, this is Martha – Mama, I want the doctor. I can't get her to move or speak. The doctor – yes, it is too early, nobody answers from the surgery. Perhaps if you know Rozhan, Dr. Kapila . . . Yes, please, as soon as you can. Pains? I don't think so. I don't know . . ."

They came and lifted her into a great high vehicle. She railed at them.

"I am not going to fly. I promised my mother I would never go into a flying boat. I have never been in a plane, never, do you know that? Nigel won't . . . Jack won't let you . . . Daddy, daddy, daddy . . ."

"She must be dreaming," they said. "Look how her lips are moving, and her arm is braced."

Basker Banerjee had come from somewhere – a great brute of a boy who used to frighten Nigel when she took him to the school sports . . . Was that little white-haired lady his granny? . . . And Rozhan, one of the schoolgirls, who had once asked why men could not be given pills to make them able to have babies – and yes, of course, the other woman was Lilian's mother. But she did not see Lilian or Angela. They were both going to be nurses. They ought to be there if she was being taken to hospital. But Angela had come on an aeroplane once with a doctor, a tall European doctor. None of the others were . . . but it didn't matter any more. Angela – they had tried to take Angela

186

away from her, but Lilian would do. Somehow Lilian was mixed up in her mind with Angela. And Lily, of course, skinny ginger Lily was her first daughter. She had not seen Lily since . . .

They prodded and pummelled her, tore off her warm clothes against silent protests, bound her under rigid blankets to the tight bed. White sheets, Martha noted, white still in the hospital as she sat beside the bed hour after hour.

They arranged a lift back for her to pick up her clothes and some woollies of Mrs. Smith's, so she moved into a neighbour's near her own house and they hired someone to keep guard back at home. The lawyer came – the young one, Councillor Mwangi's son – to see if the old lady could instruct him, but of course she couldn't: Martha could have told him that.

He patted her shoulder – him! A boy younger that Lilian – and told her he had telephoned to Nigel and not to worry. She would be all right. How could he know she would be all right? Fortunately she had some common sense and children of her own. But she felt cold, so cold, with nothing to do while they hooked her madam on to tubes and messed her about and failed to understand those few words she managed to get out.

Day after day she sat, all the hours they allowed her to, while the others fussed in and out, bringing flowers and cards and oranges and bottles which remained untouched on the bedside table. Now and again there would be a contorted whisper;

"Has Angela come?"

"For better for worse. This is for better, Jack."

"Lily, don't open your mouth till you have thought what to say . . . Meena . . . Sara . . . Parminder . . . Lily . . . Lily."

Martha would reply as best she could:

"You will see Angela soon."

"Nigel is coming."

"The girls are all doing well."

On the fifth day Nigel came. He looked bigger than ever, red-faced, tired, out of place. He came almost running up the ward, took a long look at his mother, then bent forward to kiss her. She did not stir for a few moments. Then she open-ed her eyes.

"Jack," she said, "you've come to see the baby."

He did not understand, looked around helplessly.

"It's Nigel, mother, Nigel come to see you. Ann and the kids send their love."

"Your arm is all right?"

"We are all right. I came as soon as I could. Young Mwangi phoned." Mrs. Smith closed her eyes again.

Martha had jumped to her feet. Suddenly aware of her, Nigel murmured a greeting, kissed her cheek, poured out questions about his mother.

Martha was appalled. It was not even as though she had been his ayah. She had met him first as a young man of twenty. Just like a European, she thought, making you ashamed, asking the impossible of you. The things other people would reasonably demand – that you get clean the ancient ridged paint work framing the window panes or remove the stain of years from a saucepan – they do not worry about. Once they know you well enough to make their own assessment they do not blame you because the hens are not laying well or a mineral stain grows under a dripping tap. But if you avert your eyes from an unlucky sight or a soft-fried egg, eh, then you are in for it, and have never been taught what taboos of theirs you are breaking.

188

How many nights of indigestion had she suffered for failing to refuse Mrs. Banerjee's sweetmeats? But one must not be rude. And there is no shame any more.

"Shall I get a room ready for you?"

She could not call him Nigel: Sir was too formal.

"No, no," he said. "I haven't hired a car. I can go to a hotel or something. How do you get on and out, Martha? I suppose there are buses now or, what do you call 'm, matatus."

"The matatu stop is two kilometres from the house. I have been staying in town. But you will need . . ."

She paused, not daring to say what he would need to do.

"Not now, Martha, not yet, it is too much . . . I don't know how to thank you for all you've done. She wouldn't come away with us, you see. And work . . . Don't worry. You will be all right."

Indeed she saw. How blessed you were when work coincided with what needed to be done, not only with what people pay for! Growing things matter most: she had learned that early on. So there was no need to be thanked. But how could he know she would be all right? Unless he meant to take over the old home and keep her working there.

At lunch-time the doctor came, and the lawyer, and they went off in a huddle to the Club. There they ran into the bank manager, who had been one of Nigel's fellow cashiers in Nairobi all those years ago, and he insisted on Nigel's staying with his family as long as they needed to be near the hospital.

"Your mother taught two of my younger sisters," he said, "and they loved her. I didn't make the connection at first, Smith being such a common name."

"You must know my colleague Opondo," Nigel said later to Martha. "He even came to Kitale for my wedding."

But Martha, though she did not remind him, had not been at the wedding.

In a couple of days more, it was over, so gently you would hardly notice the change. The lips had moved sometimes, and the eyes had shown fear, excitement, acquiescence, but veiled themselves against the last sleep.

Basker Banerjee drove them out to the old house and Martha busied herself packing together her own things, not bearing to watch Nigel as he confronted the old home. He did not take much – some photographs, childhood books, Uncle's medals and a few pieces of jewellery for Ann. Bidden to help herself, Martha took a few familiar pots and pans, the glass-topped tray and the cashmere sweater Lily Beach had brought. They bundled up the books for the school library and the old clothes for the Salvation Army. The lawyer would dispose of the house and furniture. Mrs. Banerjee had suggested they set aside a few mementoes for old friends, and Martha was glad, afterwards, that this had not been forgotten. Some of the settlement people filed in to shake hands with Nigel and give him pole, and he told Njoroge's nephew to take away the remaining chickens. Then he bit his lip and turned away.

Martha sat in the church, wearing the big hat she had had for Lilian's wedding, with Nigel and Councillor Mwangi and Mrs. Banerjee and Mrs. Mistri. A dozen old girls and a few old boys from the school turned up. Paddy had sent an apology from Kitale saying he could not get about too well these days. Felix Kimalel had left his garage to come, and the vicar surprised them by saying he had visited the farm long ago when his uncle Njoroge was head-man there, and had found Mrs. Smith calling at the staff

190

quarters and speaking Swahili correctly. This was unexpe-
cted because he seemed such a high class sort of man.

Martha rented a room while she sorted herself out. It
was like the move to the new village, wondering how you
will get through the years ahead. Mr. Mwangi told her to
keep the post office key till the rental expired because he
would be writing to her. He also told Nigel that an Old
Cambrian school dinner would be coming up in a few days –
Matthew was on the committee: he might as well look up
some old friends there in Nairobi while his flight to Australia was being booked.

Chapter *10*

Martha leaned against the gate to get her breath. It was a low iron gate with bars that would let cats or dogs or vermin in and a noisy latch that had no place for a padlock. The little square between her and the front door was covered with more concrete than grass, and there were plaster figures set about it that recalled her vision of idols in the Old Testament. The sky was pale and the pavements were a clean pale grey and the pale children were chattering and larking on their way home from school. The older ones wore drab uniforms of grey or navy blue, but the little ones were allowed what clothes the parents chose and Ted, now nine years old, waved to her cheerfully, "Hi, Gran!" out of a yellow checked windcheater and long trousers. His cheeks were fat and shiny brown, his voice exactly echoed his father's. She had tried to teach them to call her Cucu but this seemed to the children beyond all reason. "Shoo-shoo- shoo," Janet and Ian mimicked, driving imaginary flocks before them and explaining that schoolmates would laugh at them unbearably. It was bad enough for Ted to bear the middle name Kimani (Kim, he explained, these days was for girls) and for the others Lilian had not insisted. She was tired of coaching the family to get their tongues round Nay-yam-boo-ra.

Martha followed her grandson into the house and began to make the tea. She was well used to English tea. Lilian would not be home yet from her duty at the clinic. Auxiliary nurse, they called her, and she never so much as gave an injection. Into her 30s and only three children: her age-mates in Kenya would be sisters or tutors in smart blue dresses, not demeaned by an apron, walking with

192

authority, their bottoms sticking out even if their bellies had achieved a constant size.

One evening Mrs. Johnson from the corner had come in to ask Lilian's advice about her hot flushes.

"Just call her Pat, mum," Lilian advised. "Johnson's about as common as Kamau and there's a whole clan of them round here."

The TV was on and Lily Beach ranting about something or other.

"You might have called Lilian after her," said Pat suddenly. "Must be getting on for sixty that one, for all those expensive outfits are meant to hide it. Got up like Lady Muck, but my granny used to buy cabbages off her mum, that I can tell you."

"She came to stay with us at home once," said Martha slowly. "A nice lady, I thought. Mrs. Smith had been her teacher once. It must have been after you came here, Lilian."

Pat's face flushed with excitement.

"You mean to say that Lily Beach actually stayed with you and went on your TV?"

"Perhaps she did. I never saw the TV in a private house till I came here," said Martha.

Pat's face fell again.

"But what did you do without the telly . . . ?"

"I was a servant, I had plenty to do," answered Martha stiffly, and then rebuked herself. "And we lived in a farm- house, you see. There was always chickens to see to and vegetables and firewood, even after the fields were sold. And we had the wireless."

"But where did Lily Beach make her speeches then, and get her hair done and all that?"

"Well, it was after Uhuru," replied Martha weakly. "We do have things nice in Kenya, you know. You could get everything you wanted if you could afford it . . . She wanted me to tell her about girls' education and how widows managed and why we weren't paid every week: that sort of thing."

"Not paid every week? Everybody is paid every week, except the top bosses."

"Oh no, we're not. Once a month is better, you see. How could you get a term's school fees or a new dress if you had all those little amounts to spend on just food and soap?"

At this point Jim came in, having been knocked out of the darts tournament at the pub.

"Lily Beach?" he exclaimed. "Poor little rich girl always on the side of the down and outs. What would she make of an all-woman world. I'd like to know? Bit of a backhander that would be – women all in power and nobody to wiggle her ass at."

Martha was glad to withdraw and go to bed. The world was topsyturvy. That nice girl all alone and she, a widow, sitting at table with her son-in-law and shutting her eyes to rest them against the colour TV.

She slept well. July in England was not colder than July in Tumutumu, and the children were quiet by eight o'clock at night. The road was quiet too, only houses in it and the cars slipped along the tarmac, seldom hooting or disputing. Public vehicles did not pass at night and the pub was two corners away. A few birds sang in the more promising gardens, a cat occasionally howled. No cocks,

194

no cows, no clatter of milk-cans or tractors. Only the TVs too loud sometimes and the kids' record players on Saturday nights..

She was to go to see Madam's two sisters and some shadowy cousin of Nigel's father. It would give her a chance to run through a bit of the country, Jim said, and they would get some peace of mind out of meeting her. How was that, if they had never stirred to come to Kenya? Well, she had borne ten years separation from Lilian. Lilian wrote letters and sent photographs, which was more than William did. It had seemed impossible she would ever be able to afford to come and see them, till the lawyer explained the settlement to her after Mrs. Smith died. But the sisters were older than Mrs. Smith, perhaps too old to travel, too desolate to have a son to send. She knew the addresses but it was Nigel who had set the correspondence in hand.

Mrs. Instone – Aunt Beatrice, Angela used to call her – was seventy three and lived in a home for retired ladies near Beaconsfield. Jim drove her down there one Saturday and they stopped for lunch at a motel on the way. Lilian had said it would not do to take the children.

"Tea with her Highness will be quite enough," Jim said. "I can tell some of the old dears will be swimming in their soup. Puts me off, that kind of thing."

Martha was not likely to be put off. But remembering places where her father had cooked – the high tinny voices, the spotless napkins, the endless range of cutlery – she kept her own counsel about Retired Ladies. From India too, they said. She had seen some of those long ago.

Mrs. Instone was taller than Mrs. Smith had been, with grey hair beautifully arranged and grey garments that were still fluttery, like her wedding pictures in the album. Apart from liver spots, she did not show her age, receiving them among the high-backed chintz chairs of the lounge where other ladies dozed or munched sweets, waiting for their weekend visitors.

"So kind of you, Mr. Carter, to bring Martha all this way to see me."

"Mrs. Kimani is my mother-in-law, Mrs. Instone. Any friend of hers is a friend of mine."

A head or two roused itself from the deep cushions and made a rapid inspection. Mrs. Instone lived up to her colours and did not blench. A skinny Pakistani hand was setting out cups on a serving table. A guttural Viennese voice chattered to what might have been granddaughters in leotards and wellington boots.

"I know what a comfort you were to my sister, Martha." Recalling her great days, Beatrice spoke loud and clearly. "I shall never cease to be grateful to the domestic staff who were like a family to me when my children were small in India. Those were happy days. How I should have liked my sister to share them! But all good things come to an end, sooner for us, more tragically for her. How did she bear up in the last days?"

"She was comfortable, madam, comfortable enough and enjoyed her food. I just had to help her with her clothes a bit, you know, and get her to use the wheel-chair outside the house in case she should fall, for her legs were stiff. Only her memory, you see . . ."

"She did not know people?"

"She recognised people she saw, and I think she knew when you and Nigel were writing to her I had mostly to read the letters. Excuse me for that. When some of the

196

Indian lady teachers came they would read them again, in case I had got anything wrong. Only she never could take in what happened to Angela. She used to sit at the gate waiting for Angela to come. So I would read my daughter's letters, only leaving out about the children. You see, Lilian is a nurse too. I did not like to deceive her madam, but I could not satisfy her any other way."

"Ah, sad, sad, but you did your best. And you must be very glad that your daughter is doing so well, with her family." *Beatrice managed a smile in Jim's direction.*

"They owe a lot to Mrs. Smith, madam. If she had not given me work, I do not know how I should have got Lilian through high school. It was not so common for girls among us in those days."

"You speak good English yourself."

"I have got a bit used to it, madam. I had only four years in school but it stood me in good stead, and in our place girls were encouraged to speak."

Martha came away feeling some sympathy with Mrs. Instone, a memsahib of the old school living cheek by jowl with shapeless old women who spilt their crumbs and dripped mucus on to the polished tables, as she herself would doubtless come to do. She would not admit that the children did not want her, but indicated that the husband and wife did not come up to her standard. That could be true enough.

Martha remembered the snowy curtains and heavy furniture of those old colonial houses before people had got around to admitting (so her father had explained) that coffee would no longer cover the cost of transporting it. Then came a time when her father had had to wash as well as cook, and his Bwana locked away the best glasses, for there was no more wine or whisky to put in them, and the memsahib went to work as a hairdresser three days a week "because she was so bored at home". The young ones might make the place pretty with plastic tablecloths and linoleum, but the memsahib would never be happy in it again.

Martha would once have thought it odd to live all together with your agemates, but remembering William's wife she partly understood and pitied Mrs. Instone in a way Mrs. Smith never needed to be pitied.

"What a life!" exclaimed Jim suddenly. "A lot of hollow shells together producing a moaning noise. You wouldn't let that happen to you, would you, mother?"

"I hope not." Slowly she produced a speech she had been putting against some such occasion. "You are good to welcome me here, Jim. Of course I am going back in September. I have a lot of things to see to. It cannot always be easy for you either. But I feel more at home in your house than in my son William's. I want you to know that."

"And welcome too. Kids ought to know their grannies. My mum, you see, died of cancer before she was fifty. One reason I went to Kenya. Couldn't bear to see my old man going to pieces. He married again and we don't see much of them. Had a few words over Lily. Now and again I take the children to see him at the club, but his wife doesn't come. Well, everybody got his own life . . ."

"I hope . . . I mean, do you think it is Lilian's fault?"

"Not a bit of it. We have our ups and downs like anyone else. I admit I didn't let her go to see you when she wanted to, after Janet was born. I was afraid she would get home-sick and not want to come back. A mate of mine married a German girl and she did that to him – went off

198

with the baby to visit her mother and never came back. Lil couldn't see it my way. Said the English had no family feeling and all that. But then Ian came along pretty fast, so there was no question of paying for all of them. Only since Ian started baby school she's gone back to work – she wanted to before, but I'd have been ashamed, you see, if people thought I couldn't look after my own – so maybe if things go well we'll save enough to come and visit you in a couple of years' time."

"That will be nice. But you think she gets on all right with the other women?"

"Oh sure, well enough. If you look a bit different you may easily take offence at what is just somebody's ordinary manner. At first she used to get a bit uptight, especially when it was the wrong time of the month, maybe."

(This is a man talking to his mother-in-law! Martha shuddered but kept her face unmoved. After all, enough taboos had been broken in Kikuyuland in times past.)

"Kikuyu women are used to talking a bit loud," she ventured. (At home it suited nurses, imposing authority, giving orders. Perhaps here was different.)

"Not only them, mother, not only them. Only some of those from the West Indies talk extra soft, coaxing, like. No, it takes all sorts – and Britain is taking all sorts in recent years, as you see for yourself. Bit of a facer for Mrs. Instone and her like, but it's made things easier for Lil, you see. We get along."

The next week Lilian was to take her mother down to Southsea on the train to see Mavis, Mrs. Downer. It would be a good outing for the children and they could walk along the front while gran made her visit.

Jim said when he was little you used to go to the seaside in the summer – for a week if you could afford it, if not, for day trips on an excursion ticket. Nowadays it was out of fashion: people flew off somewhere abroad or else went to country pubs at some fancy price, visiting stately homes and all that. A day on the coach was quite enough for her and Jim could go off on a football weekend with some of his mates and leave her to get on with her work at home. But she wouldn't mind having a look at this Southsea place.

Martha thought over what she had to say, what photographs to take with her . . . She had no expectations of the seaside. She had never been to Mombasa, where Stephen had got lost, and, looking down from the aeroplane, the crinkled surface said to be water aroused no images in her. She had seen Lake Nakuru, of course, in the old days when you could stroll down to the edge and pick up the flamingo feathers, but now it was all fenced off and you had to pay. From the bus it appeared just a sheet of tin bordered at certain seasons with a hazy pink.

The week weighed on her. Dusting when Lilian was out at work, watching the meaningless TV programmes which little Ian could mimic so well, trotting after Lilian round the supermarkets. They were ten times the size of those she was used to and sold countless varieties of the same thing – Irish butter, Danish butter, enriched butter, creamery butter instead of just butter. Five weeks till she would be getting home and overhauling the house and checking on her land application. During that time they were going to have their two-week holiday and take her on trips. Lilian asked if she would like to fly to Amsterdam to see the Hypermarket. She shuddered at the

*explanation. Jim was right in thinking she would prefer
an old English country market out of doors. They had
bought her a raincoat and stockings and a woolly scarf,
but she herself was not at ease in the shops. She had
brought from home a toy jiko set for Janet and carved
animals for the boys, but there was no charcoal for the
jiko and they had amazing toys that could walk or squeak
or clatter about. She bought paper hats for William's
children and a spongebag for his wife. Nobody seemed to
sell necessities in Greater London. Perhaps everybody had
them already.*

*Mrs. Downer was about seventy. Her husband had
died but she carried on the boarding-house in partnership
with her sister-in-law. "I'd be glad to see her, but tell her
not to expect too much," she had written to Nigel. What
did that mean? Martha began to understand as they
strolled along the sea front: chains, railings and ·kiosks
had a dilapidated air and there were dingy shops which
Lilian had to shoo the children away from.*

*The boarding-house was in good repair on the outside
but the interior was drearily familiar to Martha – thread
bare rugs, furniture worn beyond polishing, curtains that
could be made to last so long as you did not wash them.
Mrs. Downer led them to a sitting-room dominated by the
inevitable TV set and then popped into the kitchen to ask
an elderly black lady to make tea.*

*"Ah, Florrie, thank you. I expect you'd like to meet our
guests: Mrs. Kimani from Kenya, where my poor sister
was, and her daughter Mrs. Carter and her kiddies. Mrs.
Coleman is our right hand here, since Rita and I are
getting a bit too stiff to do all we used to. Time was we
had two people living in and extra in the summer, but*

now we put it all onto her or I don't know what we'd do. Have a cup, Florrie?"

"No thanks, my love," said Florrie gently. "You want to hear about your sister, I know, and I'm behind with the dishes already. I think you're in my line of country, Mrs. Kimani, and you have to keep regular hours, don't you? It's a blessing the poor soul had you to look after her."

Lilian and the children tactfully followed Florrie out.

"You don't mind if I call you Martha? That's what Ellen always used to call you. I'm Mavis. I'm older than she was. It seems ridiculous that she should have gone first. Three years since I had a letter from her, but the lady from the school always told me you kept her comfortable. It's not easy: I know myself, though for my hubby it wasn't that long. Did she . . . I mean it was never my impression that Jack did much for her even when he was alive. Was it too depressing for her, really?"

Martha glanced around seeking an answer, and Mavis understood.

"Well, as you get older you don't mind so much the look of things. My sister Beatrice does, perhaps, but then we were never good enough for her. Rita and I cater for the students and such. Married people don't go for furnished rooms anymore now: it's so easy to get every-thing on credit – not to say you don't know who is married any longer. So we give them breakfast and clean up their rooms a bit, otherwise they'd be no way of keeping them fit for the health inspector.

"Well, that's all by the way . . . She was eating all right?"

"Till the last weeks, yes, madam – Mavis, I mean. It got a bit messy but then we all come to it, don't we? She

202

was only the last week in hospital, and the doctor kept her sleepy – I couldn't let go the chance he might do something for her."

"Of course you couldn't. And Nigel came?"

"Just in time, yes. It was Angela she never got over – whether she really didn't know or closed her mind to it, I couldn't say, but she was always expecting Angela to walk in . . ."

Both women sat, constrained, looking at where, in their youth, the fireplace would have been.

"There are some photographs – I thought . . . a china jug she used to be fond of . . . perhaps you would like . . ."

"Thank you. It is strange getting old, isn't it? Everything fades. You know it is nearly thirty years since I saw her. You did well to come and visit your daughter. If I had been braver – Africa, you see, it always seemed to frighten us. And then to take the time, let alone the money. Beatrice thought you could lord over it in Kenya like India, but India beat her in the end . . . Your husband, Martha? My sister told me you were a widow bringing up children. Did you nurse him too?"

"Nurse him? Oh no, oh no. Lilian was eight years old then and my baby was hardly two. He was coming home to visit us – we were still in the homestead then; we had not moved to the new villages . . . He died on the way. He never arrived."

"You mean there was a road accident?"

"No – no accident. He was cut – quite badly cut, people said. We could never be sure. Those were bad times, you see."

"Bad indeed, but who . . .? Did you get compensation? The children . . ."

"In those days you did not ask who or why. I did not even know where he stayed in the city. We did not get his clothes or anything. But I had a girl and two boys – two others I had lost before William was born – so you have to keep on, don't you?"

They were at the airport too early, not being habitual travellers. Ian was tearing around, frustrated at not being able to see the planes. Ted was listing all the places he would like to go to, Janet trying hard to concentrate on her ideas of Africa.

A bustle aroused them, of flashing cameras, a slim red-haired lady of indeterminate age, dressed in exquisite casuals, accompanied by perfect light-weight bags on rollers (a fat lot of use those would be in a Kenyan town), quickfire answers to questions . . .

"There's your old friend Lily Beach, mother," hissed Jim.

So indeed it was.

"And perhaps she doesn't know . . ."

To their amazement Martha was on her feet and shouting, "Miss Beach, Miss Beach . . ."

In the turmoil nobody seemed to notice. They were going to weigh in the baggage.

"Excuse me, excuse me. Lily . . . Lily . . ."

The mountain voice did its work. Lily Beach turned and surveyed the crowd.

"It's me, madam, Martha, where you stayed with Mrs. Smith."

"Smith?" (Of course she remembered, as common as Kimani.)

"Mrs. Smith in Kenya, madam, who was your teacher . . . I thought, you will excuse me ladies, perhaps you did not know that Mrs. Smith died a few months ago. Pardon me, but I thought you would like to know."

"Martha – why, of course, Martha – you had – yes, you had a daughter by my name . . . Here? Now? But how marvellous. Lily, look me up when I come back from India. Here's my card – they are all afraid I am going to miss the flight . . . Look, one of you hand over my papers for me . . . No, I didn't·know she died. Miss Mountford, she did a lot for me . . . You looked after her until . . .? Well, yes, of course you did. An English lady, that's what she always seemed to me when I was a schoolgirl. And then to see her like that thirty years afterwards, so absorbed, so . . · . belonging. Can you tell me when she changed?"

"Changed, madam, Lily, I mean? Well, no, we are all getting older of course. But my madam – Mrs. Smith, mama Nigel – no I wouldn't say that any of us has changed."

www.ingramcontent.com/pod-product-compliance
Lightning Source LLC
Chambersburg PA
CBHW070536100726
47907CB00004B/1143